Adventures of Gerard

Sir Arthur Conan Doyle was born in Edinburgh in 1859 of an Irish Catholic family. He was educated at Stonyhurst and Edinburgh University where he qualified as a doctor, and afterwards practised at Southsea from 1882 to 1890.

There can be few men in history and even fewer writers whose genius had so many facets, and few can have received so many sincere tributes from men of all nations. His influence on police methods and criminology all over the world is well known. In his Sherlock Holmes stories he originated the use of plaster of Paris for preserving delicate clues; the examination of dust from clothes for identification; the analysis of the different qualities of various tobacco ashes; and, of course, the now universally accepted science of deduction. The Chinese and Egyptian police used Conan Doyle's works as their official training text books; J. Edgar Hoover, as its chief, declared that the FBI had incorporated his methods to the full; and the French Sûreté named its celebrated criminal laboratory at Lyons after him.

The range of his books is immense. The fame of Sherlock Holmes tends to overshadow his historical novels (though these are considered to be among his finest and most enduring work), his vast output of short stories, his official history of the Boer War and six-volume history of the Great War. A list of his achievements, too long to give in full, is astounding: he invented the Naval life-jacket, persuaded the Army to adopt the steel helmet and before World War I warned in vain of the menace of U-boats. He worked in close association with Sir Winston Churchill in the Pilgrim Trust and was as warmly admired in the United States as in Britain and France.

He played both football and cricket for his county; and once played for the Gentlemen of England. He was one of England's team in the Prince Henry Motor Race in 1911 – another example of the pioneering spirit that always inspired him. He was an expert boxer and billiards player, and it was he who introduced skiing into Switzerland in 1893.

When he died in 1930, one of his greatest contemporaries, Sir Winston Churchill, said of him: 'I had a great admiration for him. Of course I read every Sherlock Holmes story. But the ~~books I enjoyed~~ more than the detective stories ~~were his historical novels. Apart from~~ Sherlock Holmes, h~~e has a secure place in~~ English literature.'

D1334120

Previously published by
Sir Arthur Conan Doyle in Pan Books

Adventures of Gerard

Sir Arthur Conan Doyle

with an Introduction by Elizabeth Longford

Pan Books London and Sydney

First published 1903 by George Newnes
This edition first published 1976 by
John Murray (Publishers) Ltd and Jonathan Cape Ltd
Published in paperback 1977 by
Pan Books Ltd, Cavaye Place, London SW10 9PG
Introduction © Elizabeth Longford 1976
The works of Sir Arthur Conan Doyle are published
by arrangement with the owners of the copyright,
Baskervilles Investments Ltd
ISBN 0 330 24846 4
Printed and bound in Great Britain by
Cox and Wyman Ltd, London, Reading and Fakenham

Contents

Introduction

The gusto and innocence of a golden age permeate the 'Napoleonic' stories of Conan Doyle. This collection, the last in the series, comes to us like Wordsworth's vision of childhood, 'trailing clouds of glory'. Adventures are thrilling, even gory, without in any way suggesting horror and violence as we know them today. Sex is imperious and delightful – how should it be otherwise in the life of a gallant Frenchman? – but it requires only the flash of a woman's eye or the flutter of her long black lashes to tell Gerard that she loves him; no need even to kiss more than her hand.

Not that the heroines of these adventures are all alike and equally compliant. Venetian Lucia in the first story is a romantic and genuine love; the pale and refined Lady Jane Dacre in England turns out to love another; Sophie on the retreat from Moscow is an evanescent but invaluable conquest; Marie, 'a stout, red-faced' Belgian woman cooking cutlets over a hot fire is bewitched for Gerard's purposes during the Battle of Waterloo by sheer Gallic tongue-in-cheek: 'Surely, it is impossible that anyone so beautiful can also be hard-hearted?' Then there are the seductive memories of the past, Dolores of Toledo, the brunette at Santarem, and Agnes whose location is not specified – all contributing in their own way to Brigadier Gerard's necessary glow of childlike self-glorification. It may have been the excitement of his exploits which held Brigadier Gerard's French audience spellbound round the table in his favourite Parisian café. But it was the praise and admiration lavished upon them which meant everything to Gerard himself. As he put it: 'All the remarkable exploits which have won me the love of so many beautiful women, and the respect of so many noble men . . .'

Perhaps my impression of this gusto and innocence comes

partly from the time at which I first discovered the *Adventures*. World War I had not long ended and I was in the midst of a glorious spring holiday from school. The dell in the garden was full of blue anemones in flower. It was hot enough to lie on the grass and read. As a schoolgirl, I was more absorbed by the horses which Brigadier Gerard rode than by the women he loved. There was Voltigeur and there was Violette, and of course Napoleon's white Arab, on which Gerard sped from the field of Waterloo disguised as the emperor, in order to deflect the pursuit from his beloved leader to himself. I remember raging inwardly at the martyrdom of horses in wars. I thought of one particular contemporary picture, very popular in World War I, of a trooper tending his wounded horse. Sir Arthur Conan Doyle may have had some of the same feelings, for he published his *Adventures of Gerard* in 1903, a year after the stubborn and heroic Boers at last surrendered to Britain. The Boer War was separated by nearly ninety years from Waterloo and by only fifteen years from Passchendaele. But in many respects the Boer War was more like the duel in the Peninsula of 1809–1814 than the muddy deadlock of 1918; for instance, in the role of cavalry and guerrillas.

On re-reading the *Adventures of Gerard* I was surprised and enchanted to find how well the animation, pace, suspense, characterization and humour had worn. Brigadier Gerard, we are reminded, is a veteran of Napoleon's *Grande Armée* who has fought his way up in the famous 'Hussars of Conflans' to become at last their Colonel. It is his pleasure in old age to spin his yarns to younger friends. There he sits in his charmed circle, leaning forward in a comfortable cane chair, a bare-headed old man in his shirtsleeves and waistcoat with a white moustache and glass of wine at his elbow. While he talks a lighted taper is held up in his right hand. But this light, which throws his shadow behind him on to the café wall, must be magical. For the shadow is that of a young, handsome Hussar officer in dolman and peaked shako with stiff upright plume, holding aloft his sabre. (That in fact is a description of the jacket produced by John

Murray for the seventh edition of the *Adventures* some forty years ago.)

The first of these adventures, his cronies are told, took place in Venice when Gerard was Marshal Suchet's 'galloper'. A gondolier, black with rage over Napoleon's theft of the bronze Horses of St Mark's in 1797, captured the unsuspecting Gerard and delivered him over to the torturers. Before he could effect the first of many hair-breadth escapes, Gerard gave his ear for his lady-love. As far as I know, this is the only physical sacrifice which he made for the ladies. That he never found it necessary to give his life for love or even his right arm, but only an ear, is somehow characteristic of the special flavour which enhances Gerard's adventures. Cynical would be too heavy a word for something so light-hearted. One might say that his adventures are never quite straightforward. There is always a twist, an undertone or overtone, which make a confidential appeal to the adult reader, so to speak, while youth at the same time is most generously served.

In the second story we move to the Peninsular War, with the siege of Saragossa (1808–9). It has a deservedly authentic ring despite Gerard's invented dénouement. For Conan Doyle had studied the sources with care. In his own Preface he named the various French military memoirs from which he had gained 'an understanding of the Napoleonic soldier', notably *Les Cahiers du Capitaine Coignet* and *Les Mémoires du Sergeant Bourgoyne*. Not only did these genuine warriors beget the imaginary Brigadier Gerard, but also André Maurois' fictional Colonel Bramble and Docteur O'Grady of World War I. Nor did Conan Doyle confine his studies to French memoirists. It is clear that he was well versed in the recollections which had been published by the beginning of this century of British Peninsular soldiers such as Captain Johnny Kincaid, Private Wheeler, Rifleman Harris, General Cavalier Mercer, and of course Wellington's Despatches.

The story of 'How He Captured Saragossa' brings out the dashing Gerard in all his gay true colours – a Frenchman for whom *'la gloire'* is the be-all and end-all of a soldier's life. As the Duke of Wellington pointed out, while the stern call of duty spurred on the Englishman to glorious deeds, the direct search for glory inspired the Frenchman. 'That is the difference', said the Duke, 'between the French and English soldier; with the French, glory is the cause; with us, the result.'

Gerard's naïve boastfulness, which is soon to become so familiar and endearing a feature of his make-up, is introduced by Conan Doyle with a skilful whiff of criticism. Thus any inclination which the reader might have to object to such self-conceit is pre-empted. When Gerard first joins the Hussars of Conflans before the walls of Saragossa, he trumpets forth their good fortune to his fellow-officers: 'Rejoice, my friends, rejoice! It is no ordinary man who has joined you tonight, but it is I, *the* Gerard, the hero of Ratisbon, the victor of Jena, the man who broke the square at Austerlitz...' The shout of incredulous laughter which greeted this pronouncement naturally forced Gerard to challenge his new comrades to a series of duels. When the time for the duels arrived, however, Gerard had already enabled the walls of Saragossa to be breached by lighting a secret fuse in a convent chapel, disguised as a monk.

'Romance nicely mixed with a right flavouring of Baron Munchhausen', has been suggested as the hall-mark of the Brigadier Gerard stories. True so far as it goes, this description perhaps fails to stress adequately the pleasant bursts of irony and rollicking humour. The third and fifth stories in this series, 'How The Brigadier Slew The Fox' and 'How He Triumphed In England', are examples of Conan Doyle at his boisterous best. In the third he has built a splendid farce out of the many English accounts of fox-hunting during the Peninsular War, in this case to while away the long winter months spent behind the lines of Torres Vedras. Mounted on a superb English hunter, Gerard rides down the hounds, hunt servants and assorted English generals, to sabre the fox with the same back-handed stroke which had earlier killed the Tsar's aide-de-camp. Far behind him he can see the outdistanced huntsmen waving their fists and yelling, as he fondly imagines, in applause. 'They are not really such a phlegmatic race, the English,' reflects Gerard complacently.

The entertaining situations inherent in the contrasts between French and English customs are carried further when Gerard arrives in Devon, a prisoner of war. At cricket he becomes a demon, anticipating the arrival of body-line bowling by some thirty years. His epic boxing match against the Honourable Baldock made me laugh out loud: first, a warning from his friend Lord Rufton, 'Mind, Gerard, no kicking!' and at the end a cry of triumph from Gerard as he butts his enemy in the stomach – 'Vive l'Empereur!'

There is much to enjoy in Gerard's adventures both among the guerrillas of the Peninsula (1810) and the Russians around Minsk during the French retreat from Moscow (1812). Conan Doyle has not hesitated to show a fictional guerrilla leader (the Smiler) as a monster of cruelty. Undoubtedly this is how the guerrillas appeared to the French; to Wellington's army they were noble patriots. It is interesting to find Gerard employing in this story a method of transport which had actually but inadvertently been used by one of Wellington's soldiers in Portugal. But if I gave the game away at this stage Gerard would be sadly disappointed in my English sportsmanship.

'Gamesmanship' rather than sportsmanship is the word that seems to sum up Gerard's debonair yet cunning attitude to life. The word has come too late for him to use, but the idea is implicit in all his exploits. It is there above all during that last long day of his life as an active soldier, a double-barrelled saga of Waterloo.

Part I opens with a typically Gerard-esque explanation of France's failure at that supreme test.

So high was the spirit of France at that time that every other spirit would have quailed before it; but these people, these English, have neither spirit nor soul, but only solid, immovable beef, against which we broke ourselves in vain. That was it, my friends! On the one side, poetry, gallantry, self-sacrifice – all that is beautiful and heroic. On the other side, beef. Our hopes, our ideals, our dreams – all were shattered on that terrible beef of Old England.

Gerard at the time of Waterloo was on Napoleon's staff and had been sent personally by the Emperor on a vital cross-country mission. His orders were to make sure that Marshal Grouchy's forces, already visible to Napoleon on the edge of the forest to the east, should put on speed and attack Wellington's left flank. But alas, the advancing Prussians intercepted Gerard and prevented his message from getting through. So far as I know, this is the only occasion when Conan Doyle seriously tampers with history. For the forces which the Emperor saw on the edge of the forest were not Grouchy's Frenchmen but Blücher's Prussians, as Napoleon very well knew. When Napoleon announced during the battle 'Grouchy is here!', he was attempting to hearten his half-beaten army with a deliberate lie. But perhaps it is too much to expect Gerard's creator to deal severely with his Emperor – or possibly Conan Doyle did not know the truth, since Henri Houssaye's French masterpiece, *1815 – Waterloo*, did not appear in England until 1900.

Part Two gives a marvellously vivid picture of the French defeat and retreat. Sprinkled with thoughts and impressions which many Frenchmen must have experienced, it should be read by anyone who wants to *feel* the Battle of Waterloo from the French angle. 'There is an old proverb,' remembers Gerard sadly, 'that in attack the French are more than men, in defeat less than women. I knew that it was true that day.'

Gerard's last mad gallop on the Emperor's white Arab is as exciting as an old silent film – *Beau Geste*, or some other heroic episode, where the silence of the film is amply filled by the cheering of the audience. Indeed, Conan Doyle's own excitement and that of his publisher's reader seem to have been so intense that they both failed to notice a sex-change in the white Arab, from horse to mare and back to horse, during the height of the chase.

Brigadier Gerard may not command the immensely wide public of Sherlock Holmes. This would no doubt deeply wound our French friend's pride. But let him rest assured of one thing. His re-birth in a new edition of the *Adventures* is a truly happy event. No one, young or old, can fail to be hilariously alive in Etienne Gerard's company.

Elizabeth Longford
1976

1 How the Brigadier lost his ear

It was the old Brigadier who was talking in the café.

I have seen a great many cities, my friends. I would not dare to tell you how many I have entered as a conqueror with eight hundred of my little fighting devils clanking and jingling behind me. The cavalry were in front of the Grande Armée, and the Hussars of Conflans were in front of the cavalry, and I was in front of the Hussars. But of all the cities which we visited Venice is the most ill-built and ridiculous. I cannot imagine how the people who laid it out thought that the cavalry could manoeuvre. It would puzzle Murat or Lasalle to bring a squadron into that square of theirs. For this reason we left Kellermann's heavy brigade and also my own Hussars at Padua on the mainland. But Suchet with the infantry held the town, and he had chosen me as his aide-de-camp for that winter, because he was pleased about the affair of the Italian fencing-master at Milan. The fellow was a good swordsman, and it was fortunate for the credit of the French arms that it was I who was opposed to him. Besides, he deserved a lesson, for if one does not like a *prima donna*'s singing one can always be silent, but it is intolerable that a public affront should be put upon a pretty woman. So the sympathy was all with me, and after the affair had blown over and the man's widow had been pensioned, Suchet chose me as his own galloper, and I followed him into Venice, where I had the strange adventure which I am about to tell you.

You have not been to Venice? No, for it is seldom that the French travel. We were great travellers in those days. From Moscow to Cairo we had travelled everywhere, but we went in larger parties than were convenient to those whom we visited, and we carried our passports in our limbers. It will be a bad day for Europe when the French start travelling again, for they are slow to leave their homes; but when they have done so no one can say how far they will go if they have a guide like our little man to point out the way. But the great days are gone and the great men are dead, and here am I, the last of them, drinking wine of Suresnes and telling old tales in a café.

But it is of Venice that I would speak. The folks there live like water-rats upon a mud-bank; but the houses are very fine, and the churches, especially that of St Mark, are as great as any I have seen. But, above all, they are all proud of their statues and their pictures, which are the most famous in Europe. There are many soldiers who think that because one's trade is to make war one should never have a thought above fighting and plunder. There was old Bouvet, for example – the one who was killed by the Prussians on the day that I won the Emperor's medal; if you took him away from the camp and the canteen, and spoke to him of books or of art, he would sit and stare at you. But the highest soldier is a man like myself who can understand the things of the mind and the soul. It is true that I was very young when I joined the army, and that the quarter-master was my only teacher; but if you go about the world with your eyes open you cannot help learning a great deal.

Thus I was able to admire the pictures in Venice, and to know the names of the great men, Michael Titiens, and Angelus, and the others, who had painted them. No one can say that Napoleon did not admire them also, for the very first thing which he did when he captured the town was to send the best of them to Paris. We all took what we could get, and I had two pictures for my share. One of them, called 'Nymphs Surprised', I kept for myself, and the other, 'Saint Barbara', I sent as a present for my mother.

It must be confessed, however, that some of our men behaved very badly in this matter of the statues and the pictures. The people at Venice were very much attached to them, and as to the four bronze horses which stood over the gate of their great church, they loved them as dearly as if they had been their children. I have always been a judge of a horse, and I had a good look at these ones, but I could not see that there was much to be said for them. They were too coarse-limbed for light cavalry chargers, and they had not the weight for the gun-teams. However, they were the only four horses, alive or dead, in the whole town, so it was not to be expected that the people would know any better. They wept bitterly when they were sent away, and ten French soldiers were found floating in the canals that night. As a punishment for these murders a great many more of their pictures were sent away, and the soldiers took to breaking the statues and firing their muskets at the stained-glass windows. This made the people furious, and there was very bad feeling in the town. Many officers and men disappeared during that winter, and even their bodies were never found.

For myself I had plenty to do, and I never found the time heavy on my hands. In every country it has been my custom to try to learn the language. For this reason I always look round for some lady who will be kind enough to teach it to me, and then we practise it together. This is the most interesting way of picking it up, and before I was thirty I could speak nearly every tongue in Europe; but it must be confessed that what you learn is not of much use for the ordinary purposes of life. My business, for example, has usually been with soldiers and peasants, and what advantage is it to be able to say to them that I love only them, and that I will come back when the wars are over?

Never have I had so sweet a teacher as in Venice. Lucia was her first name, and her second – but a gentleman forgets second names. I can say this with all discretion, that she was of one of the senatorial families of Venice, and that her grandfather had been Doge of the town. She was of an exquisite beauty – and when I, Etienne Gerard, use such a word as 'exquisite', my friends, it has a meaning. I have judgement, I have memories, I have the means of comparison. Of all the women who have loved me there are not twenty to whom I could apply such a term as that. But I say again that Lucia was exquisite. Of the dark type I do not recall her equal unless it were Dolores of Toledo. There was a little brunette whom I loved at Santarem when I was soldiering under Massena in Portugal – her name has escaped me. She was of a perfect beauty, but she had not the figure nor the grace of Lucia. There was Agnes, also. I could not put one before the other, but I do none an injustice when I say that Lucia was the equal of the best.

It was over this matter of pictures that I had first met her, for her father owned a palace on the farther side of the Rialto Bridge upon the Grand Canal, and it was so packed with wall-paintings that Suchet sent a party of sappers to cut some of them out and send them to Paris. I had gone down with them, and after I had seen Lucia in tears it appeared to me that the plaster would crack if it were taken from the support of the wall. I said so, and the sappers were withdrawn. After that I was the friend of the family, and many a flask of Chianti have I cracked with the father and many a sweet lesson have I had from the daughter. Some of our French officers married in Venice that winter, and I might have done the same, for I loved her with all my heart; but Etienne Gerard had his sword, his horse, his regiment, his mother, his Emperor and his career. A debonair Hussar has room in his heart for love, but none for a wife. So I thought then, my friends, but I did not see the lonely days when I should long to clasp those vanished hands, and turn my head away when I saw old comrades with their tall children standing round their chairs. This love which I had thought was a joke and a plaything – it is only now that I understand that it is the moulder of one's life, the most solemn and sacred of all things. . . Thank you, my friend, thank you! It is a good wine, and a second bottle cannot hurt.

And now I will tell you how my love for Lucia was the cause of one of the most terrible of all the wonderful adventures which have ever befallen me, and how it was that I came to lose the top of my right ear. You have often asked me why it was missing. Tonight for the first time I will tell you.

Suchet's headquarters at that time was the old palace of the Doge Dandolo, which stands on the lagoon not far from the place of San Marco. It was near the end of the winter, and I had returned one night from the Theatre Goldoni, when I found a note from Lucia and a gondola waiting. She prayed me to come to her at once as she was in trouble. To a Frenchman and a soldier there was but one answer to such a note. In an instant I was in the boat and the gondolier was pushing out into the dark lagoon. I remember that as I took my seat in the boat I was struck by the man's great size. He was not tall, but he was one of the broadest men that I have ever seen in my life. But the gondoliers of Venice are a strong breed, and powerful men are common enough among them. The fellow took his place behind me and began to row.

A good soldier in an enemy's country should everywhere and at all times be on the alert. It has been one of the rules of my life, and if I have lived to wear grey hairs it is because I have observed it. And yet upon that night I was as careless as a foolish young recruit who fears lest he should be thought to be afraid. My pistols I had left behind in my hurry. My sword was at my belt, but it is not always the most convenient of weapons. I lay back in my seat in the gondola, lulled by the gentle swish of the water and the steady creaking of the oar. Our way lay through a network of narrow canals with high houses towering on either side and a thin slit of star-spangled sky above us. Here and there, on the bridges which spanned the canal, there was the dim glimmer of an oil lamp, and sometimes there came a gleam from some niche, where a candle burned before the image of a saint. But save for this it was all black, and one could only see the water by the white fringe which curled round the long black nose of our boat. It was a place and a time for dreaming. I thought of my own past life, of all the great deeds in which I had been concerned, of the horses that I had handled, and of the women that I had loved. Then I thought also of my dear mother, and I fancied her joy when she heard the folk in the village talking about the fame of her son. Of the Emperor also I thought, and of France, the dear fatherland, the sunny France, mother of beautiful daughters and of gallant sons. My heart glowed within me as I thought of how we had brought her colours so many hundred leagues beyond her borders. To her greatness I would dedicate my life. I placed my hand upon my heart as I swore it, and at that instant the gondolier fell upon me from behind.

When I say that he fell upon me I do not mean merely that he attacked me, but that he really did tumble upon me with all his weight. The fellow stands behind you and above you as he rows, so that you can neither see him nor can you in any way guard against such an assault. One moment I had sat with my mind filled with sublime resolutions, the next I was flattened out upon the bottom of the boat, the breath dashed out of my body, and this monster pinning me down. I felt the fierce pants of his hot breath upon the back of my neck. In an instant he had torn away my sword, had slipped a sack over my head, and had tied a rope firmly round the outside of it. There was I at the bottom of the gondola as helpless as a trussed fowl. I could not shout, I could not move; I was a mere bundle. An instant later I heard once more the swishing of the water and the creaking of the oar. This fellow had done his work and had resumed his journey as quietly and unconcernedly as if he were accustomed to clap a sack over a colonel of Hussars every day of the week.

I cannot tell you the humiliation and also the fury which filled my mind as I lay there like a helpless sheep being carried to the butcher's. I, Etienne Gerard, the champion of the six brigades of light cavalry and the first swordsman of the Grand Army, to be overpowered by a single, un-armed man in such a fashion! Yet I lay quiet, for there is a time to resist and there is a time to save one's strength. I had felt the fellow's grip upon my arms, and knew that I would be a child in his hands. I waited quietly, therefore, with a heart which burned with rage, until my opportunity should come.

How long I lay there at the bottom of the boat I cannot tell; but it seemed to me to be a long time, and always there were the hiss of the waters and the steady creaking of the oars. Several times we turned corners, for I heard the long, sad cry which these gondoliers give when they wish to warn their fellows that they are coming. At last, after a considerable journey, I felt the side of the boat scrape up against a landing-place. The fellow knocked three times with his oar upon wood, and in answer to his summons I heard the rasping of bars and the turning of keys. A great door creaked back upon its hinges.

'Have you got him?' asked a voice, in Italian.

My monster gave a laugh and kicked the sack in which I lay.

'Here he is,' said he.

'They are waiting.' He added something which I could not understand.

'Take him, then,' said my captor. He raised me in his arms, ascended some steps, and I was thrown down upon a hard floor. A moment later the bars creaked and the key whined once more. I was a prisoner inside a house.

From the voices and the steps there seemed now to be several people round me. I understand Italian a great deal better than I speak it, and I could make out very well what they were saying.

'You have not killed him, Matteo?'

'What matter if I have?'

'My faith, you will have to answer for it to the tribunal.'

'They will kill him, will they not?'

'Yes, but it is not for you or me to take it out of their hands.'

'Tut! I have not killed him. Dead men do not bite, and his cursed teeth met in my thumb as I pulled the sack over his head.'

'He lies very quiet.'

'Tumble him out and you will find he is lively enough.'

The cord which bound me was undone and the sack drawn from over my head. With my eyes closed I lay motionless upon the floor.

'By the saints, Matteo, I tell you that you have broken his neck.'

'Not I. He has only fainted. The better for him if he never came out of it again.'

I felt a hand within my tunic.

'Matteo is right,' said a voice. 'His heart beats like a hammer. Let him lie and he will soon find his senses.'

I waited for a minute or so and then I ventured to take a stealthy peep from between my lashes. At first I could see nothing, for I had been so long in darkness and it was but a dim light in which I found myself. Soon, however, I made out that a high and vaulted ceiling covered with painted gods and goddesses was arching over my head. This was no mean den of cut-throats into which I had been carried, but it must be the hall of some Venetian palace. Then, without movement, very slowly and stealthily I had a peep at the men who surrounded me. There was the gondolier, a swart, hard-faced, murderous ruffian, and beside him were three other men, one of them a little, twisted fellow with an air of authority and several keys in his hand, the other two tall young servants in a smart livery. As I listened to their talk I saw that the small man was the steward of the house, and that the others were under his orders.

There were four of them, then, but the little steward might be left out of the reckoning. Had I a weapon I should have smiled at such odds as those. But, hand to hand, I was no match for the one even without three others to aid him. Cunning, then, not force, must be my aid. I wished to look round for some mode of escape, and in doing so I gave an almost imperceptible movement of my head. Slight as it was it did not escape my guardians.

'Come, wake up, wake up!' cried the steward.

'Get on your feet, little Frenchman,' growled the gondolier. 'Get up, I say!' and for the second time he spurned me with his foot.

Never in the world was a command obeyed so promptly as that one. In an instant I had bounded to my feet and rushed as hard as I could run to the back of the hall. They were after me as I have seen the English hounds follow a fox, but there was a long passage down which I tore. It turned to the left and again to the left, and then I found myself back in the hall once more. They were almost within touch of me and there was no time for thought. I turned towards the staircase, but two men were coming down it. I dodged back and tried the door through which I had been brought, but it was fastened with great bars and I could not loosen them. The gondolier was on me with his knife, but I met him with a kick on the body which stretched him on his back. His dagger flew with a clatter across the marble floor. I had no time to seize it, for there were half a dozen of them now clutching at me. As I rushed through them the little steward thrust his leg before me and I fell with a crash, but I was up in an instant, and breaking from their grasp I burst through the very middle of them and made for a door at the other end of the hall. I reached it well in front of them, and I gave a shout of triumph as the handle turned freely in my hand, for I could see that it led to the outside and that all was clear for my escape. But I had forgotten this strange city in which I was. Every house is an island. As I flung open the door, ready to bound out into the street, the light of the hall shone upon the deep, still, black water which lay flush with the topmost step. I shrank back, and in an instant my pursuers were on me. But I am not taken so easily.

Again I kicked and fought my way through them, though one of them tore a handful of hair from my head in his effort to hold me. The little steward struck me with a key and I was battered and bruised, but once more I cleared a way in front of me. Up the grand staircase I rushed, burst open the pair of huge folding doors which faced me, and learned at last that my efforts were in vain.

The room into which I had broken was brilliantly lighted. With its gold cornices, its massive pillars, and its painted walls and ceilings it was evidently the grand hall of some famous Venetian palace. There are many hundred such in this strange city, any one of which has rooms which would grace the Louvre or Versailles. In the centre of this great hall there was a raised daïs, and upon it in a half circle there sat twelve men all clad in black gowns, like those of a Franciscan monk, and each with a mask over the upper part of his face.

A group of armed men – rough-looking rascals – were standing round the door and, amid them, facing the daïs was a young fellow in the uniform of the light infantry. As he turned his head I recognized him. It was Captain Auret, of the 7th, a young Basque with whom I had drunk many a glass during the winter. He was deadly white, poor wretch, but he held himself manfully amid the assassins who surrounded him. Never shall I forget the sudden flash of hope which shone in his dark eyes when he saw a comrade burst into the room, or the look of despair which followed as he understood that I had come not to change his fate but to share it.

You can think how amazed these people were when I hurled myself into their presence. My pursuers had crowded in behind me and choked the doorway, so that all further flight was out of the question. It is at such instants that my nature asserts itself. With dignity I advanced towards the tribunal. My jacket was torn, my hair dishevelled, my head was bleeding, but there was that in my eyes and in my carriage which made them realize that no common man was before them. Not a hand was raised to arrest me until I halted in front of a formidable old man whose long grey beard and masterful manner told me that both by years and by character he was the man in authority.

'Sir,' said I, 'you will perhaps tell me why I have been forcibly arrested and brought to this place. I am an honourable soldier, as is this other gentleman here, and I demand that you will instantly set us both at liberty.'

There was an appalling silence to my appeal. It is not pleasant to have twelve masked faces turned upon you and to see twelve pairs of vindictive Italian eyes fixed with fierce intentness upon your face. But I stood as a debonair soldier should, and I could not but reflect how much credit I was bringing upon the Hussars of Conflans by the dignity of my bearing. I do not think that anyone could have carried himself better under such difficult circumstances. I looked with a fearless face from one assassin to another, and I waited for some reply.

It was the greybeard who at last broke the silence.

'Who is this man?' he asked.

'His name is Gerard,' said the little steward at the door.

'Colonel Gerard,' said I. 'I will not deceive you. I am Etienne Gerard, *the* Colonel Gerard, five times mentioned in despatches and recommended for the sword of honour. I am aide-de-camp to General Suchet, and I demand my instant release, together with that of my comrade in arms.'

The same terrible silence fell upon the assembly, and the same twelve pairs of merciless eyes were bent upon my face. Again it was the greybeard who spoke.

'He is out of his order. There are two names upon our list before him.'

'He escaped from our hands and burst into the room.'

'Let him await his turn. Take him down to the wooden cell.'

'If he resists us, your excellency?'

'Bury your knives in his body. The tribunal will uphold you. Remove him until we have dealt with the others.'

They advanced upon me and for an instant I thought of resistance. It would have been a heroic death, but who was there to see it or to chronicle it? I might be only postponing my fate, and yet I had been in so many bad places and come out unhurt that I had learned always to hope and to trust my star. I allowed these rascals to seize me, and I was led from the room, the gondolier walking at my side with a long naked knife in his hand. I could see in his brutal eyes the satisfaction which it would give him if he could find some excuse for plunging it into my body.

They are wonderful places, these great Venetian houses, palaces and fortresses and prisons all in one. I was led along a passage and down a bare stone stair until we came to a short corridor from which three doors opened. Through one of these I was thrust and the spring lock closed behind me. The only light came dimly through a small grating which opened on the passage. Peering and feeling, I carefully examined the chamber in which I had been placed. I understood from what I had heard that I should soon have to leave it again in order to appear before this tribunal, but still it is not my nature to throw away any possible chances.

The stone floor of the cell was so damp and the walls for some feet high were so slimy and foul that it was evident that they were beneath the level of the water. A single slanting hole high up near the ceiling was the only aperture for light or air. Through it I saw one bright star shining down upon me, and the sight filled me with comfort and with hope. I have never been a man of religion, though I have always had a respect for those who were, but I remember that night that the star shining down the shaft seemed to be an all-seeing eye which was upon me, and I felt as a young and frightened recruit might feel in battle when he saw the calm gaze of his colonel turned upon him.

Three of the sides of my prison were formed of stone, but the fourth was of wood, and I could see that it had only recently been erected. Evidently a partition had been thrown up to divide a single large cell into two smaller ones. There was no hope for me in the old walls, in the tiny window, or in the massive door. It was only in this one direction of the wooden screen that there was any possibility of exploring. My reason told me that if I should pierce it – which did not seem very difficult – it would only be to find myself in another cell as strong as that in which I then was. Yet I had always rather be doing something than doing nothing, so I bent all my attention and all my energies upon the wooden wall. Two planks were badly joined and so loose that I was certain I could easily detach them. I searched about for some tool, and I found one in the leg of a small bed which stood in the corner. I forced the end of this into the chink of the planks, and I was about to twist them outwards when the sound of rapid footsteps caused me to pause and listen.

I wish I could forget what I heard. Many a hundred men have I seen die in battle, and I have slain more myself than I care to think of, but all that was fair fight and the duty of a soldier. It was a very different matter to listen to a murder in this den of assassins. They were pushing someone along the passage, someone who resisted and who clung to my door as he passed. They must have taken him into the third cell, the one which was farthest from me. 'Help! help!' cried a voice, and then I heard a blow and a scream. 'Help! help!' cried the voice again, and then 'Gerard! Colonel Gerard!' It was my poor captain of infantry whom they were slaughtering. 'Murderers! murderers!' I yelled, and I kicked at my door, but again I heard him shout, and then everything was silent. A minute later there was a heavy splash, and I knew that no human eye would ever see Auret again. He had gone as a hundred others had gone whose names were missing from the roll-calls of their regiments during that winter in Venice.

The steps returned along the passage, and I thought that they were coming for me. Instead of that they opened the door of the cell next to mine, and they took someone out of it. I heard the steps die away up the stair. At once I renewed my work upon the planks, and within a very few minutes I had loosened them in such a way that I could remove and replace them at pleasure. Passing through the aperture I found myself in the farther cell, which, as I expected, was the other half of the one in which I had been confined. I was not any nearer to escape than I had been before, for there was no other wooden wall which I could penetrate, and the spring lock of the door had been closed. There were no traces to show who was my companion in misfortune. Closing the two loose planks behind me, I returned to my own cell, and waited there with all the courage which I could command for the summons which would probably be my death-knell.

It was a long time in coming, but at last I heard the sound of feet once more in the passage, and I nerved myself to listen to some other odious deed and to hear the cries of the poor victim. Nothing of the kind occurred, however, and the prisoner was placed in the cell without violence. I had no time to peep through my hole of communication, for next moment my own door was flung open and my rascally gondolier, with the other assassins, came into the cell.

'Come, Frenchman,' said he. He held his blood-stained

knife in his great hairy hand, and I read in his fierce eyes that he only looked for some excuse in order to plunge it into my heart. Resistance was useless. I followed without a word. I was led up the stone stair and back into that gorgeous chamber in which I had left the secret tribunal. I was ushered in, but to my surprise it was not on me that their attention was fixed. One of their own number, a tall, dark young man, was standing before them and was pleading with them in low, earnest tones. His voice quivered with anxiety and his hands darted in and out or writhed together in an agony of entreaty. 'You cannot do it! You cannot do it!' he cried. 'I implore the tribunal to reconsider this decision.'

'Stand aside, brother,' said the old man who presided. 'The case is decided and another is up for judgement.'

'For Heaven's sake be merciful!' cried the young man.

'We have already been merciful,' the other answered. 'Death would have been a small penalty for such an offence. Be silent and let judgement take its course.'

I saw the young man throw himself in an agony of grief into his chair. I had no time, however, to speculate as to what it was which was troubling him, for his eleven colleagues had already fixed their stern eyes upon me. The moment of fate had arrived.

'You are Colonel Gerard?' said the terrible old man.

'I am.'

'Aide-de-camp to the robber who calls himself General Suchet, who in turn represents that arch-robber Buonaparte?'

It was on my lips to tell him that he was a liar, but there is a time to argue and a time to be silent.

'I am an honourable soldier,' said I. 'I have obeyed my orders and done my duty.'

The blood flushed into the old man's face and his eyes blazed through his mask.

'You are thieves and murderers, every man of you,' he cried. 'What are you doing here? You are Frenchmen. Why are you not in France? Did we invite you to Venice? By what right are you here? Where are our pictures? Where are the horses of St Mark? Who are you that you should pilfer those treasures which our fathers through so many centuries have collected? We were a great city when France was a desert. Your drunken, brawling, ignorant soldiers have undone the work of saints and heroes. What have you to say to it?'

He was, indeed, a formidable old man, for his white beard bristled with fury and he barked out the little sentences like a savage hound. For my part I could have told him that his pictures would be safe in Paris, that his horses were really not worth making a fuss about, and that he could see heroes – I say nothing of saints – without going back to his ancestors or even moving out of his chair. All this I could have pointed out, but one might as well argue with a Mameluke about religion. I shrugged my shoulders and said nothing.

'The prisoner has no defence,' said one of my masked judges.

'Has anyone any observation to make before judgement is passed?' The old man glared round him at the others.

'There is one matter, your excellency,' said another. 'It can scarce be referred to without reopening a brother's wounds, but I would remind you that there is a very particular reason why an exemplary punishment should be inflicted in the case of this officer.'

'I had not forgotten it,' the old man answered. 'Brother, if the tribunal has injured you in one direction, it will give you ample satisfaction in another.'

The young man who had been pleading when I entered the room staggered to his feet.

'I cannot endure it,' he cried. 'Your excellency must forgive me. The tribunal can act without me. I am ill! I am mad!' He flung his hands up with a furious gesture and rushed from the room.

'Let him go! Let him go!' said the president. 'It is, indeed, more than can be asked of flesh and blood that he should remain under this roof. But he is a true Venetian, and when the first agony is over he will understand that it could not be otherwise.'

I had been forgotten during this episode, and though I am not a man who is accustomed to being overlooked I should have been all the happier had they continued to neglect me. But now the old president glared at me again like a tiger who comes back to his victim.

'You shall pay for it all, and it is but justice that you should,' said he. 'You, an upstart adventurer and foreigner, have dared to raise your eyes in love to the grand-daughter of a Doge of Venice who was already betrothed to the heir of the Loredans. He who enjoys such privileges must pay a price for them.'

'It cannot be higher than they are worth,' said I.

'You will tell us that when you have made a part payment,' he said. 'Perhaps your spirit may not be so proud by that time. Matteo, you will lead this prisoner to the wooden cell. Tonight is Monday. Let him have no food or water, and let him be led before the tribunal again on Wednesday night. We shall then decide upon the death which he is to die.'

It was not a pleasant prospect, and yet it was a reprieve. One is thankful for small mercies when a hairy savage with a blood-stained knife is standing at one's elbow. He dragged me from the room and I was thrust down the stairs and back into my cell. The door was locked and I was left to my reflections.

My first thought was to establish connection with my neighbour in misfortune. I waited until the steps had died away, and then I cautiously drew aside the two boards and peeped through. The light was very dim, so dim that I could only just discern a figure huddled in the corner, and I could hear the low whisper of a voice which prayed as one prays who is in deadly fear. The boards must have made a creaking. There was a sharp exclamation of surprise.

'Courage, friend, courage!' I cried. 'All is not lost. Keep a stout heart, for Etienne Gerard is by your side.'

'Etienne!' It was a woman's voice which spoke – a voice

which was always music to my ears. I sprang through the gap and I flung my arms round her. 'Lucia! Lucia!' I cried.

It was 'Etienne!' and 'Lucia!' for some minutes, for one does not make speeches at moments like that. It was she who came to her senses first.

'Oh, Etienne, they will kill you. How came you into their hands?'

'In answer to your letter.'

'I wrote no letter.'

'The cunning demons! But you?'

'I came also in answer to your letter.'

'Lucia, I wrote no letter.'

'They have trapped us both with the same bait.'

'I care nothing about myself, Lucia. Besides, there is no pressing danger with me. They have simply returned me to my cell.'

'Oh, Etienne, Etienne, they will kill you. Lorenzo is there.'

'The old greybeard?'

'No, no, a young dark man. He loved me, and I thought I loved him until – until I learned what love is, Etienne. He will never forgive you. He has a heart of stone.'

'Let them do what they like. They cannot rob me of the past, Lucia. But you – what about you?'

'It will be nothing, Etienne. Only a pang for an instant and then all over. They mean it as a badge of infamy, dear, but I will carry it like a crown of honour since it was through you that I gained it.'

Her words froze my blood with horror. All my adventures were insignificant compared to this terrible shadow which was creeping over my soul.

'Lucia! Lucia!' I cried. 'For pity's sake tell me what these butchers are about to do. Tell me, Lucia! Tell me!'

'I will not tell you, Etienne, for it would hurt you far more than it would me. Well, well, I will tell you lest you should fear it was something worse. The president has ordered that my ear be cut off, that I may be marked for ever as having loved a Frenchman.'

Her ear! The dear little ear which I had kissed so often. I put my hand to each little velvet shell to make certain that this sacrilege had not yet been committed. Only over my dead body should they reach them. I swore it to her between my clenched teeth.

'You must not care, Etienne. And yet I love that you should care all the same.'

'They shall not hurt you – the fiends!'

'I have hopes, Etienne. Lorenzo is there. He was silent while I was judged, but he may have pleaded for me after I was gone.'

'He did. I heard him.'

'Then he may have softened their hearts.'

I knew that it was not so, but how could I bring myself to tell her? I might as well have done so, for with the quick instinct of woman my silence was speech to her.

'They would not listen to him! You need not fear to tell me, dear, for you will find that I am worthy to be loved by such a soldier. Where is Lorenzo now?'

'He left the hall.'

'Then he may have left the house as well.'

'I believe that he did.'

'He has abandoned me to my fate. Etienne, Etienne, they are coming!'

Afar off I heard those fateful steps and the jingle of distant keys. What were they coming for now, since there were no other prisoners to drag to judgement? It could only be to carry out the sentence upon my darling. I stood between her and the door, with the strength of a lion in my limbs. I would tear the house down before they should touch her.

'Go back! Go back!' she cried. 'They will murder you, Etienne. My life, at least, is safe. For the love you bear me, Etienne, go back. It is nothing. I will make no sound. You will not hear that it is done.'

She wrestled with me, the delicate creature, and by main force she dragged me to the opening between the cells. But a sudden thought had crossed my mind.

'We may yet be saved,' I whispered. 'Do what I tell you at once and without argument. Go into my cell. Quick!'

I pushed her through the gap and helped her to replace the planks. I had retained her cloak in my hands, and with this wrapped round me I crept into the darkest corner of her cell. There I lay when the door was opened and several men came in. I had reckoned that they would bring no lantern, for they had none with them before. To their eyes I was only a black blur in the corner.

'Bring a light,' said one of them.

'No, no; curse it!' cried a rough voice, which I knew to be that of the ruffian Matteo. 'It is not a job that I like, and the more I saw it the less I should like it. I am sorry, signora, but the order of the tribunal has to be obeyed.'

My impulse was to spring to my feet and to rush through them all and out by the open door. But how would that help Lucia? Suppose that I got clear away, she would be in their hands until I could come back with help, for single-handed I could not hope to clear a way for her. All this flashed through my mind in an instant, and I saw that the only course for me was to lie still, take what came, and wait my chance. The fellow's coarse hand felt about among my curls – those curls in which only a woman's fingers had ever wandered. The next instant he gripped my ear, and a pain shot through me as if I had been touched with a hot iron. I bit my lip to stifle a cry, and I felt the blood run warm down my neck and back.

'There, thank Heaven that's over,' said the fellow, giving me a friendly pat on the head. 'You're a brave girl, signora, I'll say that for you, and I only wish you'd have better taste than to love a Frenchman. You can blame him and not me for what I have done.'

What could I do save to lie still and grind my teeth at my own helplessness? At the same time my pain and my rage were always soothed by the reflection that I had suffered for the woman whom I loved. It is the custom of men to say to ladies that they would willingly endure any pain for their sake, but it was my privilege to show that I had said no more than I meant. I thought also how nobly I would seem to have acted if ever the story came to be told, and how proud the regiment of Conflans might well be of their colonel. These thoughts helped me to suffer in silence while the blood still trickled over my neck and dripped upon the stone floor. It was that sound which nearly led to my destruction.

'She's bleeding fast,' said one of the valets. 'You had best fetch a surgeon or you will find her dead in the morning.'

'She lies very still and she's never opened her mouth,' said another. 'The shock has killed her.'

'Nonsense; a young woman does not die so easily.' It was Matteo who spoke. 'Besides, I did but snip off enough to leave the tribunal's mark upon her. Rouse up, signora, rouse up!'

He shook me by the shoulder, and my heart stood still for fear he should feel the epaulette under the mantle.

'How is it with you now?' he asked.

I made no answer.

'Curse it! I wish I had to do with a man instead of a woman, and the fairest woman in Venice,' said the gondolier. 'Here, Nicholas, lend me your handkerchief and bring a light.'

It was all over. The worst had happened. Nothing could save me. I still crouched in the corner, but I was tense in every muscle, like a wild cat about to spring. If I had to die I was determined that my end should be worthy of my life.

One of them had gone for a lamp, and Matteo was stooping over me with a handkerchief. In another instant my secret would be discovered. But he suddenly drew himself straight and stood motionless. At the same instant there came a confused murmuring sound through the little window far above my head. It was the rattle of oars and the buzz of many voices. Then there was a crash upon the door upstairs, and a terrible voice roared: 'Open! Open in the name of the Emperor!'

The Emperor! It was like the mention of some saint which, by its very sound, can frighten the demons. Away they ran with cries of terror – Matteo, the valets, the steward, all of the murderous gang. Another shout and then the crash of a hatchet and the splintering of planks. There were the rattle of arms and the cries of French soldiers in the hall. Next instant feet came flying down the stair and a man burst frantically into my cell.

'Lucia!' he cried. 'Lucia!' He stood in the dim light, panting and unable to find his words. Then he broke out again. 'Have I not shown you how I love you, Lucia ? What more could I do to prove it ? I have betrayed my country, I have broken my vow, I have ruined my friends, and I have given my life in order to save you.'

It was young Lorenzo Loredan, the lover whom I had superseded. My heart was heavy for him at the time, but after all it is every man for himself in love, and if one fails in the game it is some consolation to lose to one who can be a graceful and considerate winner. I was about to point this out to him, but at the first word I uttered he gave a shout of astonishment, and, rushing out, he seized the lamp which hung in the corridor and flashed it in my face.

'It is you, you villain!' he cried. 'You French coxcomb. You shall pay me for the wrong which you have done me.'

But the next instant he saw the pallor of my face and the blood which was still pouring from my head.

'What is this ?' he asked. 'How come you to have lost your ear ?'

I shook off my weakness and, pressing my handkerchief to my wound, I rose from my couch, the debonair colonel of Hussars.

'My injury, sir, is nothing. With your permission we will not allude to a matter so trifling and so personal.'

But Lucia had burst through from her cell and was pouring out the whole story while she clasped Lorenzo's arm.

'This noble gentleman – he has taken my place, Lorenzo! He has borne it for me. He has suffered that I might be saved.'

I could sympathize with the struggle which I could see in the Italian's face. At last he held out his hand to me.

'Colonel Gerard,' he said, 'you are worthy of a great love. I forgive you, for if you have wronged me you have made a noble atonement. But I wonder to see you alive. I left the tribunal before you were judged, but I understood that no mercy would be shown to any Frenchman since the destruction of the ornaments of Venice.'

'He did not destroy them,' cried Lucia. 'He has helped to preserve those in our palace.'

'One of them, at any rate,' said I, as I stooped and kissed her hand.

This was the way, my friends, in which I lost my ear. Lorenzo was found stabbed to the heart in the Piazza of St Mark within two days of the night of my adventure. Of the tribunal and its ruffians, Matteo and three others were shot, the rest banished from the town. Lucia, my lovely Lucia, retired into a convent at Murano after the French had left the city, and there she still may be, some gentle lady abbess who has perhaps long forgotten the days when our hearts throbbed together, and when the whole great world seemed so small a thing beside the love which burned in our veins. Or perhaps it may not be so. Perhaps she has not forgotten. There may still be times when the peace of the cloister is broken by the memory of the old soldier who loved her in those distant days. Youth is past and passion is gone, but the soul of the gentleman can never change, and still Etienne Gerard would bow his grey head before her and would very gladly lose this other ear if he might do her a service.

2 How the Brigadier captured Saragossa

Have I ever told you, my friends, the circumstances connected with my joining the Hussars of Conflans at the time of the siege of Saragossa, and the very remarkable exploit which I performed in connection with the taking of that city? No? Then you have indeed something still to learn. I will tell it to you exactly as it occurred. Save for two or three men and a score or two of women, you are the first who have ever heard the story.

You must know, then, that it was in the 2nd Hussars – called the Hussars of Chamberan – that I served as a lieutenant and as a junior captain. At the time I speak of I was only twenty-five years of age, as reckless and desperate a man as any in that great army. It chanced that the war had come to a halt in Germany, while it was still raging in Spain; so the Emperor, wishing to reinforce the Spanish army, transferred me as senior captain to the Hussars of Conflans, which were at that time in the 5th Army Corps under Marshal Lannes.

It was a long journey from Berlin to the Pyrenees. My new regiment formed part of the force which, under Marshal Lannes, was then besieging the Spanish town of Saragossa. I turned my horse's head in that direction, therefore, and behold me a week or so later at the French headquarters, whence I was directed to the camp of the Hussars of Conflans.

You have read, no doubt, of this famous siege of Saragossa, and I will only say that no general could have had a harder task than that with which Marshal Lannes was confronted. The immense city was crowded with a horde of Spaniards – soldiers, peasants, priests – all filled with the most furious hatred of the French, and the most savage determination to perish before they would surrender. There were eighty thousand men in the town and only thirty thousand to besiege them. Yet we had a powerful artillery, and our Engineers were of the best. There was never such a siege, for it is usual that when the fortifications are taken the city falls; but here it was not until the fortifications were taken that the real fighting began. Every house was a fort and every street a battlefield, so that slowly, day by day, we had to work our way inwards, blowing up the houses with their garrisons until more than half the city had disappeared. Yet the other half was as determined as ever, and in a better position for defence, since it consisted of enormous convents and monasteries with walls like the Bastille, which could not be so easily brushed out of our way. This was the state of things at the time that I joined the army.

I will confess to you that cavalry are not of much use in a siege, although there was a time when I would not have permitted anyone to have made such an observation. The Hussars of Conflans were encamped to the south of the town, and it was their duty to throw out patrols and to make sure that no Spanish force was advancing from that quarter. The colonel of the regiment was not a good soldier, and the regiment was at that time very far from being in the high condition which it afterwards attained. Even in that one evening I saw several things which shocked me; for I had a high standard, and it went to my heart to see an ill-arranged camp, an ill-groomed horse, or a slovenly trooper. That night I supped with twenty-six of my new brother-officers, and I fear that in my zeal I showed them only too plainly that I found things very different to what I was accustomed to in the army of Germany. There was silence in the mess after my remarks, and I felt that I had been indiscreet when I saw the glances that were cast at me. The colonel especially was furious, and a great major named Olivier, who was the fire-eater of the regiment, sat opposite to me curling his huge black moustaches, and staring at me as if he would eat me. However, I did not resent his attitude, for I felt that I had indeed been indiscreet, and that it would give a bad impression if upon this my first evening I quarrelled with my superior officer.

So far I admit that I was wrong, but now I come to the sequel. Supper over, the colonel and some other officers left the room, for it was in a farmhouse that the mess was held. There remained a dozen or so, and a goat-skin of Spanish wine having been brought in, we all made merry. Presently this Major Olivier asked me some questions concerning the army of Germany and as to the part which I had myself played in the campaign. Flushed with wine, I was drawn on from story to story. It was not unnatural, my friends. You will sympathise with me. Up there I had been the model for every officer of my years in the army. I was the first swordsman, the most dashing rider, the hero of a hundred adventures. Here I found myself not only unknown, but even disliked. Was it not natural that I should wish to tell these brave comrades what sort of man it was that had come among them ? Was it not natural that I should wish to say, 'Rejoice, my friends, rejoice! It is no ordinary man who has joined you tonight, but it is I, *the* Gerard, the hero of Ratisbon, the victor of Jena, the man who broke the square at Austerlitz' ? I could not say all this. But I could at least tell them some incidents which would enable them to say it for themselves. I did so. They listened unmoved. I told them more. At last, after my tale of how I had guided the army across the Danube, one universal shout of laughter broke from them all. I sprang to my feet, flushed with shame and anger. They had drawn me on. They were making game of me. They were convinced that they had to do with a braggart and a liar. Was this my reception in the Hussars of Conflans ? I dashed the tears of mortification from my eyes, and they laughed the more at the sight.

'Do you know, Captain Pelletan, whether Marshal Lannes is still with the army ?' asked the major.

'I believe that he is, sir,' said the other.

'Really, I should have thought that his presence was hardly necessary now that Captain Gerard has arrived.'

Again there was a roar of laughter. I can see the ring of faces, the mocking eyes, the open mouths – Olivier with his great black bristles, Pelletan thin and sneering, even the young sub-lieutenants convulsed with merriment. Heavens, the indignity of it! But my rage had dried my tears. I was myself again, cold, quiet, self-contained, ice without and fire within.

'May I ask, sir,' said I to the major, 'at what hour the regiment is paraded?'

'I trust, Captain Gerard, that you do not mean to alter our hours,' said he, and again there was a burst of laughter, which died away as I looked slowly round the circle.

'What hour is the assembly?' I asked, sharply, of Captain Pelletan.

Some mocking answer was on his tongue, but my glance kept it there. 'The assembly is at six,' he answered.

'I thank you,' said I. I then counted the company, and found that I had to do with fourteen officers, two of whom appeared to be boys fresh from St Cyr. I could not condescend to take any notice of their indiscretion. There remained the major, four captains, and seven lieutenants.

'Gentlemen,' I continued, looking from one to the other of them, 'I should feel myself unworthy of this famous regiment if I did not ask you for satisfaction for the rudeness with which you have greeted me, and I should hold you to be unworthy of it if on any pretext you refused to grant it.'

'You will have no difficulty upon that score,' said the major. 'I am prepared to waive my rank and to give you every satisfaction in the name of the Hussars of Conflans.'

'I thank you,' I answered. 'I feel, however, that I have some claim upon these other gentlemen who laughed at my expense.'

'Whom would you fight, then?' asked Captain Pelletan.

'All of you,' I answered.

They looked in surprise from one to the other. Then they drew off to the other end of the room, and I heard the buzz of their whispers. They were laughing. Evidently they still thought that they had to do with some empty braggart. Then they returned.

'Your request is unusual,' said Major Olivier, 'but it will

be granted. How do you propose to conduct such a duel? The terms lie with you.'

'Sabres,' said I. 'And I will take you in order of seniority, beginning with you, Major Olivier, at five o'clock. I will thus be able to devote five minutes to each before the assembly is blown. I must, however, beg you to have the courtesy to name the place of meeting, since I am still ignorant of the locality.'

They were impressed by my cold and practical manner. Already the smile had died away from their lips. Olivier's face was no longer mocking, but it was dark and stern.

'There is a small open space behind the horse lines,' said he. 'We have held a few affairs of honour there, and it has done very well. We shall be there, Captain Gerard, at the hour you name.'

I was in the act of bowing to thank them for their acceptance when the door of the mess-room was flung open and the colonel hurried into the room, with an agitated face.

'Gentlemen,' said he, 'I have been asked to call for a volunteer from among you for a service which involves the greatest possible danger. I will not disguise from you that the matter is serious in the last degree, and that Marshal Lannes has chosen a cavalry officer because he can be better spared than an officer of infantry or of Engineers. Married men are not eligible. Of the others, who will volunteer?'

I need not say that all the unmarried officers stepped to the front. The colonel looked round in some embarrassment. I could see his dilemma. It was the best man who should go, and yet it was the best man whom he could least spare.

'Sir,' said I, 'may I be permitted to make a suggestion?'

He looked at me with a hard eye. He had not forgotten my observations at supper. 'Speak!' said he.

'I would point out, sir,' said I, 'that this mission is mine both by right and by convenience.'

'Why so, Captain Gerard?'

'By right, because I am the senior captain. By convenience, because I shall not be missed in the regiment, since the men have not yet learned to know me.'

The colonel's features relaxed.

'There is certainly truth in what you say, Captain Gerard,' said he. 'I think that you are indeed best fitted to go upon this mission. If you will come with me I will give you your instructions.'

I wished my new comrades good night as I left the room, and I repeated that I should hold myself at their disposal at five o'clock next morning. They bowed in silence, and I thought that I could see, from the expression of their faces, that they had already begun to take a more just view of my character.

I had expected that the colonel would at once inform me what it was that I had been chosen to do, but instead of that he walked on in silence, I following behind him. We passed through the camp and made our way across the trenches and over the ruined heaps of stones which marked the old wall of the town. Within there was a labyrinth of passages, formed among the débris of the houses which had been destroyed by the mines of the Engineers. Acres and acres were covered with splintered walls and piles of brick which had once been a populous suburb. Lanes had been driven through it and lanterns placed at the corners with inscriptions to direct the wayfarer. The colonel hurried onwards until at last, after a long walk, we found our way barred by a high grey wall which stretched right across our path. Here behind a barricade lay our advanced guard. The colonel led me into a roofless house, and there I found two general officers, a map stretched over a drum in front of them, they kneeling beside it and examining it carefully by the light of a lantern. The one with the clean-shaven face and the twisted neck was Marshal Lannes, the other was General Razout, the head of the Engineers.

'Captain Gerard has volunteered to go,' said the colonel.

Marshal Lannes rose from his knees and shook me by the hand.

'You are a brave man, sir,' said he. 'I have a present to make to you,' he added, handing me a very tiny glass tube. 'It has been specially prepared by Dr Fardet. At the supreme moment you have but to put it to your lips and you will be dead in an instant.'

This was a cheerful beginning. I will confess to you, my friends, that a cold chill passed up my back and my hair rose upon my head.

'Excuse me, sir,' said I, as I saluted, 'I am aware that I have volunteered for a service of great danger, but the exact details have not yet been given to me.'

'Colonel Perrin,' said Lannes severely, 'it is unfair to allow this brave officer to volunteer before he has learned what the perils are to which he will be exposed.'

But already I was myself once more.

'Sir,' said I, 'permit me to remark that the greater the danger the greater the glory, and that I could only repent of volunteering if I found that there were no risks to be run.'

It was a noble speech, and my appearance gave force to my words. For the moment I was an heroic figure. As I saw Lannes's eyes fixed in admiration upon my face it thrilled me to think how splendid was the début which I was making in the army of Spain. If I died that night my name would not be forgotten. My new comrades and my old, divided in all else, would still have a point of union in their love and admiration of Etienne Gerard.

'General Razout, explain the situation!' said Lannes, briefly.

The Engineer officer rose, his compasses in his hand. He led me to the door and pointed to the high grey wall which towered up amongst the débris of the shattered houses.

'That is the enemy's present line of defence,' said he. 'It is the wall of the great Convent of the Madonna. If we can carry it the city must fall, but they have run counter-mines all round it, and the walls are so enormously thick that it would be an immense labour to breach it with artillery. We happen to know, however, that the enemy have a considerable store of powder in one of the lower chambers. If that could be exploded the way would be clear for us.'

'How can it be reached?' I asked.

'I will explain. We have a French agent within the town

named Hubert. This brave man has been in constant communication with us, and he had promised to explode the magazine. It was to be done in the early morning, and for two days running we have had a storming party of a thousand Grenadiers waiting for the breach to be formed. But there has been no explosion, and for these two days we have had no communication from Hubert. The question is, what has become of him?'

'You wish me to go and see?'

'Precisely. Is he ill, or wounded, or dead? Shall we still wait for him, or shall we attempt the attack elsewhere? We cannot determine this until we have heard from him. This is a map of the town, Captain Gerard. You perceive that within this ring of convents and monasteries are a number of streets which branch off from a central square. If you come so far as this square you will find the cathedral at one corner, In that corner is the street of Toledo. Hubert lives in a small house between a cobbler's and a wine-shop, on the right-hand side as you go from the cathedral. Do you follow me?'

'Clearly.'

'You are to reach that house, to see him, and to find out if his plan is still feasible or if we must abandon it.' He produced what appeared to be a roll of dirty brown flannel. 'This is the dress of a Franciscan friar,' said he. 'You will find it the most useful disguise.'

I shrank away from it.

'It turns me into a spy,' I cried. 'Surely I can go in my uniform?'

'Impossible! How could you hope to pass through the streets of the city? Remember, also, that the Spaniards take no prisoners, and that your fate will be the same in whatever dress you are taken.'

It was true, and I had been long enough in Spain to know that that fate was likely to be something more serious than mere death. All the way from the frontier I had heard grim tales of torture and mutilation. I enveloped myself in the Franciscan gown.

'Now I am ready.'

'Are you armed?'

'My sabre.'

'They will hear it clank. Take this knife and leave your sword. Tell Hubert that at four o'clock before dawn the storming party will again be ready. There is a sergeant outside who will show you how to get into the city. Good night and good luck!'

Before I had left the room the two generals had their cocked hats touching each other over the map. At the door an under-officer of Engineers was waiting for me. I tied the girdle of my gown, and taking off my busby I drew the cowl over my head. My spurs I removed. Then in silence I followed my guide.

It was necessary to move with caution, for the walls above were lined by the Spanish sentries, who fired down continually at our advanced posts. Slinking along under the very shadow of the great convent, we picked our way slowly and carefully among the piles of ruins until we came to a large chestnut tree. Here the sergeant stopped.

'It is an easy tree to climb,' said he. 'A scaling ladder would not be simpler. Go up it, and you will find that the top branch will enable you to step upon the roof of that house. After that it is your guardian angel who must be your guide, for I can help you no more.'

Girding up the heavy brown gown, I ascended the tree as directed. A half-moon was shining brightly, and the line of roof stood out dark and hard against the purple, starry sky. The tree was in the shadow of the house. Slowly I crept from branch to branch until I was near the top. I had but to climb along a stout limb in order to reach the wall. But suddenly my ears caught the patter of feet, and I cowered against the trunk and tried to blend myself with its shadow. A man was coming towards me on the roof. I saw his dark figure creeping along, his body crouching, his head advanced, the barrel of his gun protruding. His whole bearing was full of caution and suspicion. Once or twice he paused, and then came on again until he had reached the edge of the parapet within a few yards of me. Then he knelt down, levelled his musket, and fired.

I was so astonished at this sudden crash at my very elbow that I nearly fell out of the tree. For an instant I could not be sure that he had not hit me. But when I heard a deep groan from below, and the Spaniard leaned over the parapet and laughed aloud, I understood what had occurred. It was my poor, faithful sergeant who had waited to see the last of me. The Spaniard had seen him standing under the tree and had shot him. You will think that it was good shooting in the dark, but these people use *trebucos*, or blunderbusses, which are filled up with all sorts of stones and scraps of metal, so that they will hit you as certainly as I have hit a pheasant on a branch. The Spaniard stood peering down through the darkness, while an occasional groan from below showed that the sergeant was still living. The sentry looked round and everything was still and safe. Perhaps he thought that he would like to finish off this accursed Frenchman, or perhaps he had a desire to see what was in his pockets; but whatever his motive he laid down his gun, leaned forward, and swung himself into the tree. The same instant I buried my knife in his body, and he fell with a loud crashing through the branches and came with a thud to the ground. I heard a short struggle below and an oath or two in French. The wounded sergeant had not waited long for his vengeance.

For some minutes I did not dare to move, for it seemed certain that someone would be attracted by the noise. However, all was silent save for the chimes striking midnight in the city. I crept along the branch and lifted myself on to the roof. The Spaniard's gun was lying there, but it was of no service to me, since he had the powder-horn at his belt. At the same time, if it were found it would warn the enemy that something had happened, so I thought it best to drop it over the wall. Then I looked round for the means of getting off the roof and down into the city.

It was very evident that the simplest way by which I

could get down was that by which the sentinel had got up, and what this was soon became evident. A voice along the roof called 'Manuelo! Manuelo!' several times, and, crouching in the shadow, I saw in the moonlight a bearded head, which protruded from a trap-door. Receiving no answer to his summons the man climbed through, followed by three other fellows all armed to the teeth. You will see here how important it is not to neglect small precautions, for had I left the man's gun where I found it a search must have followed, and I should certainly have been discovered. As it was, the patrol saw no sign of their sentry and thought, no doubt, that he had moved along the line of the roofs. They hurried on, therefore, in that direction, and I, the instant that their backs were turned, rushed to the open trap-door and descended the flight of steps which led from it. The house appeared to be an empty one, for I passed through the heart of it and out, by an open door, into the street beyond.

It was a narrow and deserted lane, but it opened into a broader road, which was dotted with fires, round which a great number of soldiers and peasants were sleeping. The smell within the city was so horrible that one wondered how people could live in it, for during the months that the siege had lasted there had been no attempt to cleanse the streets or to bury the dead. Many people were moving up and down from fire to fire, and among them I observed several monks. Seeing that they came and went unquestioned, I took heart and hurried on my way in the direction of the great square. Once a man rose from beside one of the fires and stopped me by seizing my sleeve. He pointed to a woman who lay motionless upon the road, and I took him to mean that she was dying, and that he desired me to administer the last offices of the Church. I sought refuge, however, in the very little Latin that was left to me. '*Ora pro nobis*,' said I, from the depths of my cowl. '*Te deum laudamus. Ora pro nobis.*' I raised my hand as I spoke and pointed forwards. The fellow released my sleeve and shrank back in silence, while I, with a solemn gesture, hurried upon my way.

As I had imagined, this broad boulevard led out into the central square, which was full of troops and blazing with fires. I walked swiftly onwards, disregarding one or two people who addressed remarks to me. I passed the cathedral and followed the street which had been described to me. Being upon the side of the city which was farthest from our attack, there were no troops encamped in it, and it lay in darkness, save for an occasional glimmer in a window. It was not difficult to find the house to which I had been directed, between the wine-shop and the cobbler's. There was no light within, and the door was shut. Cautiously I pressed the latch, and I felt that it had yielded. Who was within I could not tell, and yet I must take the risk. I pushed the door open and entered.

It was pitch-dark within – the more so as I had closed the door behind me. I felt round and came upon the edge of a table. Then I stood still and wondered what I should do next, and how I could gain some news of this Hubert, in whose house I found myself. Any mistake would cost me not only my life, but the failure of my mission. Perhaps he did not live alone. Perhaps he was only a lodger in a Spanish family, and my visit might bring ruin to him as well as to myself. Seldom in my life have I been more perplexed. And then, suddenly, something turned my blood cold in my veins. It was a voice, a whispering voice, in my very ear. 'Mon Dieu!' cried the voice in a tone of agony. 'Oh, mon Dieu! mon Dieu!' Then there was a dry sob in the darkness, and all was still once more.

It thrilled me with horror, that terrible voice; but it thrilled me also with hope, for it was the voice of a Frenchman.

'Who is there?' I asked.

There was a groaning, but no reply.

'Is that you, Monsieur Hubert?'

'Yes, yes,' sighed the voice, so low that I could hardly hear it. 'Water, water, for Heaven's sake, water!'

I advanced in the direction of the sound, but only to come in contact with the wall. Again I heard a groan, but this time there could be no doubt that it was above my head. I put up my hands, but they felt only empty air.

'Where are you?' I cried.

'Here! Here!' whispered the strange, tremulous voice. I stretched my hand along the wall, and I came upon a man's naked foot. It was as high as my face, and yet, so far as I could feel, it had nothing to support it. I staggered back in amazement. Then I took a tinder-box from my pocket and struck a light. At the first flash a man seemed to be floating in the air in front of me, and I dropped the box in my amazement. Again, with tremulous fingers, I struck the flint against the steel, and this time I lit not only the tinder, but the wax taper. I held it up, and if my amazement was lessened, my horror was increased by that which it revealed.

The man had been nailed to the wall as a weasel is nailed to the door of a barn. Huge spikes had been driven through his hands and his feet. The poor wretch was in his last agony, his head sunk upon his shoulder and his blackened tongue protruded from his lips. He was dying as much from thirst as from his wounds, and these inhuman wretches had placed a beaker of wine upon the table in front of him to add a fresh pang to his tortures. I raised it to his lips. He had still strength enough to swallow, and the light came back a little to his dim eyes.

'Are you a Frenchman?' he whispered.

'Yes. They have sent me to learn what had befallen you.'

'They discovered me. They have killed me for it. But before I die let me tell you what I know. A little more of that wine, please! Quick! Quick! I am very near the end. My strength is going. Listen to me! The powder is stored in the Mother Superior's room. The wall is pierced, and the end of the train is in Sister Angela's cell, next the chapel. All was ready two days ago. But they discovered a letter, and they tortured me.'

'Good Heavens! have you been hanging here for two days?'

'It seems like two years. Comrade, I have served France, have I not? Then do one little service for me. Stab me to the heart, dear friend! I implore you, I entreat you, to put an end to my sufferings.'

The man was indeed in a hopeless plight, and the kindest action would have been that for which he begged. And yet I could not in cold blood drive my knife into his body, although I knew how I should have prayed for such a mercy had I been in his place. But a sudden thought crossed my mind. In my pocket I held that which would give an instant and painless death. It was my own safeguard against torture, and yet this poor soul was in very pressing need of it, and he had deserved well of France.

I took out my phial and emptied it into the cup of wine. I was in the act of handing it to him when I heard a sudden clash of arms outside the door. In an instant I put out my light and slipped behind the window-curtains. Next moment the door was flung open, and two Spaniards strode into the room – fierce, swarthy men in the dress of citizens, but with muskets slung over their shoulders. I looked through the chink in the curtains in an agony of fear lest they had come upon my traces, but it was evident that their visit was simply in order to feast their eyes upon my unfortunate compatriot. One of them held the lantern which he carried up in front of the dying man, and both of them burst into a shout of mocking laughter. Then the eyes of the man with the lantern fell upon the flagon of wine upon the table. He picked it up, held it, with a devilish grin, to the lips of Hubert, and then, as the poor wretch involuntarily inclined his head forward to reach it, snatched it back and took a long gulp himself. At the same instant he uttered a loud cry, clutched wildly at his own throat, and fell stone dead upon the floor. His comrade stared at him in horror and amazement. Then, overcome by his own superstitious fears, he gave a yell of terror and rushed madly from the room. I heard his feet clattering wildly on the cobble-stones until the sound died away in the distance.

The lantern had been left burning upon the table, and by its light I saw, as I came out from behind my curtain, that the unfortunate Hubert's head had fallen forward upon his chest and that he also was dead. That motion to reach the wine with his lips had been his last. A clock ticked loudly in the house, but otherwise all was absolutely still. On the wall hung the twisted form of the Frenchman, on the floor lay the motionless body of the Spaniard, all dimly lit by the horn lantern. For the first time in my life a frantic spasm of terror came over me. I had seen ten thousand men in every conceivable degree of mutilation stretched upon the ground, but the sight had never affected me like those two silent figures who were my companions in that shadowy room. I rushed into the street as the Spaniard had done, eager only to leave that house of gloom behind me, and I had run as far as the cathedral before my wits came back to me. There I stopped panting in the shadow, and, my hand pressed to my side, I tried to collect my scattered senses and to plan out what I should do. As I stood there, breathless, the great brass bells roared twice above my head. It was two o'clock. Four was the hour when the storming party would be in its place. I had still two hours in which to act.

The cathedral was brilliantly lit within, and a number of people were passing in and out; so I entered, thinking that I was less likely to be accosted there and that I might have quiet to form my plans. It was certainly a singular sight, for the place had been turned into a hospital, a refuge and a storehouse. One aisle was crammed with provisions, another was littered with sick and wounded, while in the centre a great number of helpless people had taken up their abode and had even lit their cooking fires upon the mosaic floors. There were many at prayer, so I knelt in the shadow of a pillar and I prayed with all my heart that I might have the good luck to get out of this scrape alive, and that I might do such a deed that night as would make my name as famous in Spain as it had become in Germany. I waited until the clock struck three and then I left the cathedral and made my way towards the Convent of the Madonna, where the assault was to be delivered. You will understand, you who know me so well, that I was not the man to return tamely to the French camp with the report that our agent was dead and that other means must be found of entering the city. Either I should find some means to finish his uncompleted task or there would be a vacancy for a senior captain in the Hussars of Conflans.

I passed unquestioned down the broad boulevard, which I have already described, until I came to the great stone convent which formed the outwork of the defence. It was built in a square with a garden in the centre. In this garden some hundreds of men were assembled, all armed and ready, for it was known, of course, within the town that this was the point against which the French attack was likely to be made. Up to this time our fighting all over Europe had always been done between one army and another. It was only here in Spain that we learned how terrible a thing it is to fight against a people. On the one hand there is no glory, for what glory could be gained by defeating this rabble of elderly shopkeepers, ignorant peasants, fanatical priests, excited women and all the other creatures who made up the garrison ? On the other hand there were extreme discomfort and danger, for these people would give you no rest, would observe no rules of war and were desperately earnest in their desire by hook or by crook to do you an injury. I began to realise how odious was our task as I looked upon the motley but ferocious groups who were gathered round the watch fires in the garden of the Convent of the Madonna. It was not for us soldiers to think about politics, but from the beginning there always seemed to be a curse upon this war in Spain.

However, at the moment I had no time to brood over such matters as these. There was, as I have said, no difficulty in getting as far as the convent garden, but to pass inside the convent unquestioned was not so easy. The first thing which I did was to walk round the garden, and I was soon able to pick out one large stained-glass window which must belong to the chapel. I had understood from Hubert that the Mother Superior's room in which the powder was stored was near to this, and that the train had been laid through a hole in the wall from some neighbouring cell. I must at all costs get into the convent. There was a guard at the door, and how could I get in without explanations? But a sudden inspiration showed me how the thing might be done. In the garden was a well, and beside the well were a number of empty buckets. I filled two of these and approached the door. The errand of a man who carries a bucket of water in each hand does not need to be explained. The guard opened to let me through. I found myself in a long stone-flagged corridor lit with lanterns, with the cells of the nuns leading out from one side of it. Now at last I was on the high road to success. I walked on without hesitation, for I knew by my observations in the garden which way to go for the chapel.

A number of Spanish soldiers were lounging and smoking in the corridor, several of whom addressed me as I passed. I fancy it was for my blessing that they asked, and my '*Ora pro nobis*' seemed to entirely satisfy them. Soon I had got as far as the chapel, and it was easy to see that the cell next door was used as a magazine, for the floor was all black with powder in front of it. The door was shut, and two fierce-looking fellows stood on guard outside it, one of them with a key stuck in his belt. Had we been alone it would not have been long before it would have been in my hand, but with his comrade there it was impossible for me to hope to take it by force. The cell next door to the magazine on the far side from the chapel must be the one which belonged to Sister Angela. It was half open. I took my courage in both hands, and leaving my buckets in the corridor, I walked unchallenged into the room.

I was prepared to find half a dozen fierce Spanish desperadoes within, but what actually met my eyes was even more embarrassing. The room had apparently been set aside for the use of some of the nuns, who for some reason had refused to quit their home. Three of them were within, one an elderly, stern-faced dame who was evidently the Mother Superior, the others young ladies of charming appearance. They were seated together at the far side of the room, and I saw with some amazement, by their manner and expressions, that my coming was both welcome and expected. In a moment my presence of mind had returned, and I saw exactly how the matter lay. Naturally, since an attack was about to be made upon the convent, these sisters had been expecting to be directed to some place of safety. Probably they were under vow not to quit the walls, and they had been told to remain in this cell until they had received further orders. In any case I adapted my conduct to this supposition, since it was clear that I must get them out of the room, and this would give me a ready excuse to do so. I first cast a glance at the door and observed that the key was within. I then made a gesture to the nuns to follow me. The Mother Superior asked me some question, but I shook my head impatiently and beckoned to her again. She hesitated, but I stamped my foot and called them forth in so imperious a manner that they came at once. They would be safer in the chapel, and thither I led them, placing them at the end which was farthest from the magazine. As the three nuns took their places before the altar my heart bounded with joy and pride within me, for I felt that the last obstacle had been lifted from my path.

And yet how often have I not found that this is the very moment of danger? I took a last glance at the Mother Superior, and to my dismay I saw that her piercing dark eyes were fixed, with an expression in which surprise was deepening into suspicion, upon my right hand. There were two points which might well have attracted her attention. One was that it was red with the blood of the sentinel whom I had stabbed in the tree. That alone might count for little, as the knife is as familiar as the breviary to the monks of Saragossa. But on my forefinger I wore a heavy gold ring – the gift of a German baroness whose name I may not mention. It shone brightly in the light of the altar lamp. Now, a ring upon a friar's hand is an impossibility, since they are vowed to absolute poverty. I turned quickly and made for the door of the chapel, but the mischief was done. As I glanced back I saw that the Mother Superior was already hurrying after me. I ran through the chapel door and along the corridor, but she called out some shrill warning to the two guards in front. Fortunately I had the presence of mind to call out also, and to point down the passage as if we were both pursuing the same object. Next instant I had dashed past them, sprang into the cell, slammed the heavy door, and fastened it upon the inside. With a bolt above and below and a huge lock in the centre it was a piece of timber that would take some forcing.

Even now if they had had the wit to put a barrel of gunpowder against the door I should have been ruined. It was their only chance, for I had come to the final stage of my adventure. Here at last, after such a string of dangers as few men have ever lived to talk of I was at one end of the powder train, with the Saragossa magazine at the other. They were howling like wolves out in the passage, and muskets were crashing against the door. I paid no heed to their clamour, but I looked eagerly round for that train of which Hubert had spoken. Of course, it must be at the side of the room next to the magazine. I crawled along it on my hands and knees, looking into every crevice, but no sign could I see. Two bullets flew through the door and flattened themselves against the wall. The thudding and smashing grew ever louder. I saw a grey pile in a corner, flew to it with a cry of joy, and found that it was only dust. Then I got back to the side of the door where no bullets could ever reach me – they were streaming freely into the room – and I tried to forget this fiendish howling in my ear and to think out where this train could be. It must have been carefully laid by Hubert lest these nuns should see it. I tried to imagine how I should myself have arranged it had I been in his place. My eye was attracted by a statue of St Joseph which stood in the corner. There was a wreath of leaves along the edge of the pedestal, with a lamp burning amidst them. I rushed across to it and tore the leaves aside. Yes, yes, there was a thin black line, which disappeared through a small hole in the wall. I tilted over the lamp, and threw myself on the ground. Next instant came a roar like thunder, the walls wavered and tottered around me, the ceiling clattered down from above, and over the yell of the terrified Spaniards was heard the terrific shout of the storming column of the Grenadiers. As in a dream – a happy dream – I heard it, and then I heard no more.

*

When I came to my senses two French soldiers were propping me up, and my head was singing like a kettle. I staggered to my feet and looked around me. The plaster had fallen, the furniture was scattered, and there were rents in the bricks, but no signs of a breach. In fact, the walls of the convent had been so solid that the explosion of the magazine had been insufficient to throw them down. On the other hand, it had caused such a panic among the defenders that our stormers had been able to carry the windows and throw open the doors almost without resistance. As I ran out into the corridor I found it full of troops, and I met Marshal Lannes himself, who was entering with his staff. He stopped and listened eagerly to my story.

'Splendid, Captain Gerard, splendid!' he cried. 'These facts will certainly be reported to the Emperor.'

'I would suggest to your Excellency,' said I, 'that I have only finished the work that was planned and carried out by Monsieur Hubert, who gave his life for the cause.'

'His services will not be forgotten,' said the Marshal. 'Meanwhile, Captain Gerard, it is half-past four, and you must be starving after such a night of exertion. My staff and I will breakfast inside the city. I assure you that you will be an honoured guest.'

'I will follow your Excellency,' said I. 'There is a small engagement which detains me.'

He opened his eyes.

'At this hour?'

'Yes, sir,' I answered. 'My fellow-officers, whom I never saw until last night, will not be content unless they catch another glimpse of me the first thing this morning.'

'*Au revoir*, then,' said Marshal Lannes, as he passed upon his way.

I hurried through the shattered door of the convent.

When I reached the roofless house in which we had held the consultation the night before, I threw off my gown, and I put on the busby and sabre which I had left there. Then, a Hussar once more, I hurried onwards to the grove which was our rendezvous. My brain was still reeling from the concussion of the powder, and I was exhausted by the many emotions which had shaken me during that terrible night. It is like a dream, all that walk in the first dim grey light of dawn, with the smouldering camp-fires around me and the buzz of the waking army. Bugles and drums in every direction were mustering the infantry, for the explosion and the shouting had told their own tale. I strode onwards until, as I entered the little clump of cork oaks behind the horse lines, I saw my twelve comrades waiting in a group, their sabres at their sides. They looked at me curiously as I approached. Perhaps with my powder-blackened face and my blood-stained hands I seemed a different Gerard to the young captain whom they had made game of the night before.

'Good morning, gentlemen,' said I. 'I regret exceedingly if I have kept you waiting, but I have not been master of my own time.'

They said nothing, but they still scanned me with curious eyes. I can see them now, standing in a line before me, tall men and short men, stout men and thin men; Olivier, with his warlike moustache; the thin, eager face of Pelletan; young Oudin, flushed by his first duel; Mortier, with the sword-cut across his wrinkled brow. I laid aside my busby and drew my sword.

'I have one favour to ask you, gentlemen,' said I. 'Marshal Lannes has invited me to breakfast, and I cannot keep him waiting.'

'What do you suggest?' asked Major Olivier.

'That you release me from my promise to give you five minutes each, and that you will permit me to attack you all together.' I stood upon my guard as I spoke.

But their answer was truly beautiful and truly French. With one impulse the twelve swords flew from their scabbards and were raised in salute. There they stood, the twelve of them, motionless, their heels together, each with his sword upright before his face.

I staggered back from them. I looked from one to the other. For an instant I could not believe my own eyes. They were paying me homage, these, the men who had jeered me! Then I understood it all. I saw the effect that I had made upon them and their desire to make reparation. When a man is weak he can steel himself against danger, but not against emotion. 'Comrades,' I cried, 'comrades—!' but I could say no more. Something seemed to take me by the throat and choke me. And then in an instant Olivier's arms were round me, Pelletan had seized me by the right hand, Mortier by the left, some were patting me on the shoulder, some were clapping me on the back, on every side smiling faces were looking into mine; and so it was that I knew that I had won my footing in the Hussars of Conflans.

3 How the Brigadier slew the fox

In all the great hosts of France there was only one officer towards whom the English of Wellington's army retained a deep, steady and unchangeable hatred. There were plunderers among the French, and men of violence, gamblers, duellists, and *roués*. All these could be forgiven, for others of their kidney were to be found among the ranks of the English. But one officer of Massena's force had committed a crime which was unspeakable, unheard of, abominable; only to be alluded to with curses late in the evening, when a second bottle had loosened the tongues of men. The news of it was carried back to England, and country gentlemen who knew little of the details of the war grew crimson with passion when they heard of it, and yeomen of the shires raised freckled fists to Heaven and swore. And yet who should be the doer of this dreadful deed but our friend the brigadier, Etienne Gerard, of the Hussars of Conflans, gay-riding, plume-tossing, debonair, the darling of the ladies and of the six brigades of light cavalry.

But the strange part of it is that this gallant gentleman did this hateful thing, and made himself the most unpopular man in the Peninsula, without ever knowing that he had done a crime for which there is hardly a name amid all the resources of our language. He died of old age, and never once in that imperturbable self-confidence which adorned or disfigured his character knew that so many thousand Englishmen would gladly have hanged him with their own hands. On the contrary, he numbered this adventure among those other exploits which he has given to the world, and many a time he chuckled and hugged himself as he narrated it to the eager circle who gathered round him in that humble café where, between his dinner and his dominoes, he would tell, amid tears and laughter, of that inconceivable Napoleonic past when France, like an angel of wrath, rose up, splendid and terrible, before a cowering continent. Let us listen to him as he tells the story in his own way and from his own point of view.

*

You must know, my friends (said he), that it was towards the end of the year eighteen hundred and ten that I and Massena and the others pushed Wellington backwards until we had hoped to drive him and his army into the Tagus. But when we were still twenty-five miles from Lisbon we found that we were betrayed, for what had this Englishman done but build an enormous line of works and forts at a place called Torres Vedras, so that even we were unable to get through them! They lay across the whole peninsula, and our army was so far from home that we did not dare to risk a reverse, and we had already learned at Busaco that it was no child's play to fight against these people. What could we do, then, but sit down in front of these lines and blockade them to the best of our power? There we remained for six months, amid such anxieties that Massena said afterwards that he had not one hair which was not white upon his body. For my own part, I did not worry much about our situation, but I looked after our horses, who were in great need of rest and green fodder. For the rest, we drank the wine of the country and passed the time as best we might. There was a lady at Santarem — but my lips are sealed. It is the part of a gallant man to say nothing, though he may indicate that he could say a great deal.

One day Massena sent for me, and I found him in his tent with a great plan pinned upon the table. He looked at me in silence with that single piercing eye of his, and I felt by his expression that the matter was serious. He was nervous and ill at ease, but my bearing seemed to reassure him. It is good to be in contact with brave men.

'Colonel Etienne Gerard,' said he, 'I have always heard that you are a very gallant and enterprising officer.'

It was not for me to confirm such a report, and yet it would be folly to deny it, so I clinked my spurs together and saluted.

'You are also an excellent rider.'

I admitted it.

'And the best swordsman in the six brigades of light cavalry.'

Massena was famous for the accuracy of his information.

'Now,' said he, 'if you will look at this plan you will have no difficulty in understanding what it is that I wish you to do. These are the lines of Torres Vedras. You will perceive that they cover a vast space, and you will realise that the English can only hold a position here and there. Once through the lines, you have twenty-five miles of open country which lie between them and Lisbon. It is very important to me to learn how Wellington's troops are distributed throughout that space, and it is my wish that you should go and ascertain.'

His words turned me cold.

'Sir,' said I, 'it is impossible that a colonel of light cavalry should condescend to act as a spy.'

He laughed and clapped me on the shoulder. 'You would not be a Hussar if you were not a hot-head,' said he. 'If you will listen you will understand that I have not asked you to act as a spy. What do you think of that horse ?'

He had conducted me to the opening of his tent, and there was a Chasseur who led up and down a most admirable creature. He was a dapple grey, not very tall – a little over fifteen hands perhaps – but with the short head and splendid arch of the neck which comes with the Arab blood. His shoulders and haunches were so muscular, and yet his legs so fine, that it thrilled me with joy just to gaze upon him. A fine horse or a beautiful woman, I cannot look at them un-moved, even now when seventy winters have chilled my blood. You can think how it was in the year '10.

'This,' said Massena, 'is Voltigeur, the swiftest horse in our army. What I desire is that you should start tonight, ride round the lines upon the flank, make your way across the enemy's rear, and return upon the other flank, bringing me news of his dispositions. You will wear a uniform, and will, therefore, if captured, be safe from the death of a spy.

It is probable that you will get through the lines un-challenged, for the posts are very scattered. Once through, in daylight you can outride anything which you meet, and if you keep off the roads you may escape entirely unnoticed. If you have not reported yourself by tomorrow night I will understand that you are taken, and I will offer them Colonel Petrie in exchange.'

Ah, how my heart swelled with pride and joy as I sprang into the saddle and galloped this grand horse up and down to show the marshal the mastery which I had of him! He was magnificent – we were both magnificent, for Massena clapped his hands and cried out in his delight. It was not I, but he, who said that a gallant beast deserves a gallant rider. Then, when for the third time, with my panache flying and my dolman streaming behind me, I thundered past him, I saw upon his hard old face that he had no longer any doubt that he had chosen the man for his purpose. I drew my sabre, raised the hilt to my lips in salute, and galloped on to my own quarters. Already the news had spread that I had been chosen for a mission, and my little rascals came swarm-ing out of their tents to cheer me. Ah! it brings the tears to my old eyes when I think how proud they were of their colonel. And I was proud of them also. They deserved a dashing leader.

The night promised to be a stormy one, which was very much to my liking. It was my desire to keep my departure most secret, for it was evident that if the English heard that I had been detached from the army they would naturally conclude that something important was about to happen. My horse was taken, therefore, beyond the picket line, as if for watering, and I followed and mounted him there. I had a map, a compass and a paper of instructions from the marshal, and with these in the bosom of my tunic, and a sabre at my side, I set out upon my adventure. A thin rain was falling, and there was no moon, so you may imagine that it was not very cheerful. But my heart was light at the thought of the honour which had been done me, and the glory which awaited me. This exploit should be one more in that brilliant series which was to change my sabre into a baton. Ah, how we dreamed, we foolish fellows, young, and drunk with success! Could I have foreseen that night as I rode, the chosen man of sixty thousand, that I should spend my life planting cabbages on a hundred francs a month! Oh, my youth, my hopes, my comrades! But the wheel turns and never stops. Forgive me, my friends, for an old man has his weakness.

My route, then, lay across the face of the high ground of Torres Vedras, then over a streamlet, past a farmhouse which had been burned down and was now only a landmark, then through a forest of young cork oaks, and so to the monastery of San Antonio, which marked the left of the English position. Here I turned south and rode quietly over the downs, for it was at this point that Massena thought that it would be most easy for me to find my way unobserved through the position. I went very slowly, for it was so dark that I could not see my hand in front of me. In such cases I leave my bridle loose, and let my horse pick its own way. Voltigeur went confidently forward, and I was very content to sit upon his back, and to peer about me, avoiding every light. For three hours we advanced in this cautious way, until it seemed to me that I must have left all danger behind me. I then pushed on more briskly, for I wished to be in the rear of the whole army by daybreak. There are many vineyards in these parts which in winter become open plains, and a horseman finds few difficulties in his way.

But Massena had underrated the cunning of these English, for it appears that there was not one line of defence, but three, and it was the third which was the most formidable, through which I was at that instant passing. As I rode, elated at my own success, a lantern flashed suddenly before me, and I saw the glint of polished gun-barrels and the gleam of a red coat.

'Who goes there?' cried a voice – such a voice! I swerved to the right and rode like a madman, but a dozen squirts of fire came out of the darkness, and the bullets whizzed all round my ears. That was no new sound to me, my friends, though I will not talk like a foolish conscript and say that I have ever liked it. But at least it had never kept me from thinking clearly, and so I knew that there was nothing for it but to gallop hard and try my luck elsewhere. I rode round the English picket, and then, as I heard nothing more of them, I concluded rightly that I had at last come through their defences. For five miles I rode south, striking a tinder from time to time to look at my pocket compass. And then in an instant – I feel the pang once more as my memory brings back the moment – my horse, without a sob or stagger, fell stone dead beneath me!

I had not known it, but one of the bullets from that infernal picket had passed through his body. The gallant creature had never winced nor weakened, but had gone while life was in him. One instant I was secure on the swiftest, most graceful horse in Massena's army. The next he lay upon his side, worth only the price of his hide, and I stood there that most helpless, most ungainly of creatures, a dismounted Hussar. What could I do with my boots, my spurs, my trailing sabre? I was far inside the enemy's lines. How could I hope to get back again? I am not ashamed to say that I, Etienne Gerard, sat upon my dead horse and sank my face in my hands in my despair. Already the first streaks were whitening in the east. In half an hour it would be light. That I should have won my way past every obstacle, and then at this last instant be left at the mercy of my enemies, my mission ruined, and myself a prisoner – was it not enough to break a soldier's heart?

But courage, my friends! We have these moments of weakness, the bravest of us; but I have a spirit like a slip of steel, for the more you bend it the higher it springs. One spasm of despair, and then a brain of ice and a heart of fire. All was not yet lost. I, who had come through so many hazards, would come through this one also. I rose from my horse and considered what had best be done.

And first of all it was certain that I could not get back. Long before I could pass the lines it would be broad daylight. I must hide myself for the day, and devote the next night to my escape. I took the saddle, holsters, and bridle from my poor Voltigeur, and I concealed them among some bushes, so that no one finding him could know that he was a French horse. Then, leaving him lying there, I wandered on in search of some place where I might be safe for the day. In every direction I could see camp fires upon the sides of the hills, and already figures had begun to move around them. I must hide quickly or I was lost. But where was I to hide? It was a vineyard in which I found myself, the poles of the vines still standing, but the plants gone. There was no cover there. Beside, I should want some food and water before another night had come. I hurried wildly onwards through the waning darkness, trusting that chance would be my friend. And I was not disappointed. Chance is a woman, my friends, and she has her eye always upon a gallant Hussar.

Well, then, I stumbled through the vineyard, something loomed in front of me, and I came upon a great square house with another long, low building upon one side of it. Three roads met there, and it was easy to see that this was the *posada*, or wine-shop. There was no light in the windows, and everything was dark and silent, but, of course, I knew that such comfortable quarters were certainly occupied, and probably by someone of importance. I have learned, however, that the nearer the danger may really be the safer the place, and so I was by no means inclined to trust myself away from this shelter. The low building was evidently the stable, and into this I crept, for the door was unlatched. The place was full of bullocks and sheep, gathered there, no doubt, to be out of the clutches of marauders. A ladder led to a loft, and up this I climbed, and concealed myself very snugly among some bales of hay upon the top. This loft had a small open window, and I was able to look down upon the front of the inn and also upon the road. Then I crouched and waited to see what would happen.

It was soon evident that I had not been mistaken when I had thought that this might be the quarters of some person of importance. Shortly after daybreak an English light dragoon arrived with a despatch, and from then onwards the place was in a turmoil, officers continually riding up and away. Always the same name was upon their lips: 'Sir Stapleton – Sir Stapleton.' It was hard for me to lie there with a dry moustache and watch the great flagons which were brought out by the landlord to these English officers. But it amused me to look at their fresh-coloured, clean-shaven, careless faces, and to wonder what they would think if they knew that so celebrated a person was lying so near to them. And then, as I lay and watched, I saw a sight which filled me with surprise.

It is incredible the insolence of these English! What do you suppose Milord Wellington had done when he found that Massena had blockaded him and that he could not move his army? I might give you many guesses. You might say that he had raged, that he had despaired, that he had brought his troops together and spoken to them about glory and the fatherland before leading them to one last battle. No, Milord did none of these things. But he sent a fleet ship to England to bring him a number of fox-dogs, and he with his officers settled himself down to chase the fox. It is true what I tell you. Behind the lines of Torres Vedras these mad Englishmen made the fox-chase three days in the week. We had heard of it in the camp, and now I myself was to see that it was true.

For, along the road which I have described, there came these very dogs, thirty or forty of them, white and brown, each with its tail at the same angle, like the bayonets of the Old Guard. My faith, but it was a pretty sight! And behind and amidst them there rode three men with peaked caps and red coats, whom I understood to be the hunters. After them came many horsemen with uniforms of various kinds, stringing along the road in twos and threes, talking together and laughing. They did not seem to be going above a trot, and it appeared to me that it must indeed be a slow fox which they hoped to catch. However, it was their affair, not mine, and soon they had all passed my window and were out of sight. I waited and I watched, ready for any chance which might offer.

Presently an officer, in a blue uniform not unlike that of our flying artillery, came cantering down the road – an elderly, stout man he was, with grey side-whiskers. He stopped and began to talk with an orderly officer of dragoons, who waited outside the inn, and it was then that I learned the advantage of the English which had been taught me. I could hear and understand all that was said.

'Where is the meet?' said the officer, and I thought that he was hungering for his bifstek. But the other answered him that it was near Altara, so I saw that it was a place of which he spoke.

'You are late, Sir George,' said the orderly.

'Yes, I had a court-martial. Has Sir Stapleton Cotton gone?'

At this moment a window opened, and a handsome young man in a very splendid uniform looked out of it.

'Halloa, Murray!' said he. 'These cursed papers keep me, but I will be at your heels.'

'Very good, Cotton. I am late already, so I will ride on.'

'You might order my groom to bring round my horse,' said the young general at the window to the orderly below, while the other went on down the road.

The orderly rode away to some outlying stable, and then in a few minutes there came a smart English groom with a cockade in his hat, leading by the bridle a horse – and, oh, my friends, you have never known the perfection to which a horse can attain until you have seen a first-class English hunter. He was superb: tall, broad, strong, and yet as graceful and agile as a deer. Coal black he was in colour, and his neck, and his shoulder, and his quarters, and his fetlocks – how can I describe him all to you? The sun shone upon him as on polished ebony, and he raised his hoofs in a little playful dance so lightly and prettily, while he tossed his mane and whinnied with impatience. Never have I seen such a mixture of strength and beauty and grace. I had often wondered how the English Hussars had managed to ride over the Chasseurs of the Guards in the affair at Astorga, but I wondered no longer when I saw the English horses.

There was a ring for fastening bridles at the door of the inn, and the groom tied the horse there while he entered the house. In an instant I had seen the chance which Fate had brought to me. Were I in that saddle I should be better off than when I started. Even Voltigeur could not compare with this magnificent creature. To think is to act with me. In one instant I was down the ladder and at the door of the stable. The next I was out and the bridle was in my hand. I bounded into the saddle. Somebody, the master or the man, shouted wildly behind me. What cared I for his shouts! I touched the horse with my spurs, and he bounded forward with such a spring that only a rider like myself could have sat him. I gave him his head and let him go – it did not matter to me where, so long as we left this inn far behind us. He thundered away across the vineyards, and in a very few minutes I had placed miles between myself and my pursuers. They could no longer tell, in that wild country, in which direction I had gone. I knew that I was safe, and so, riding to the top of a small hill, I drew my pencil and note-book from my pocket, and proceeded to make plans of those camps which I could see, and to draw the outline of the country.

He was a dear creature upon whom I sat, but it was not easy to draw upon his back, for every now and then his two ears would cock, and he would start and quiver with impatience. At first I could not understand this trick of his, but soon I observed that he only did it when a peculiar noise – 'Yoy, yoy, yoy' – came from somewhere among the oak woods beneath us. And then suddenly this strange cry changed into a most terrible screaming, with the frantic blowing of a horn. Instantly he went mad – this horse. His eyes blazed. His mane bristled. He bounded from the earth and bounded again, twisting and turning in a frenzy. My pencil flew one way and my note-book another. And then, as I looked down into the valley, an extraordinary sight met my eyes. The hunt was streaming down it. The fox I could not see, but the dogs were in full cry, their noses down, their tails up, so close together that they might have been one great yellow and white moving carpet. And behind them rode the horsemen – my faith, what a sight! Consider every type which a great army could show: some in hunting dress, but the most in uniforms; blue dragoons, red dragoons, red-trousered hussars, green riflemen, artillerymen, gold-slashed lancers, and most of all red, red, red, for the infantry officers ride as hard as the cavalry. Such a crowd, some well mounted, some ill, but all flying along as best they might, the subaltern as good as the general, jostling and pushing, spurring and driving, with every thought thrown to the winds save that they should have the blood of this absurd fox! Truly, they are an extraordinary people, the English! But I had little time to watch the hunt or to marvel at these islanders, for of all these mad creatures the very horse upon which I sat was the maddest. You understand that he was himself a hunter, and that the crying of these dogs was to him what the call of a cavalry trumpet in the street yonder would be to me. It thrilled him. It drove him wild. Again and again he bounded into the air, and then, seizing the bit between his teeth, he plunged down the slope, and galloped after the dogs. I swore, and tugged, and pulled, but I was powerless. This English general rode his horse with a snaffle only, and the beast had a mouth of iron. It was useless to pull him back. One might as well try to keep a Grenadier from a wine bottle. I gave it up in despair, and, settling down in the saddle, I prepared for the worst which could befall.

What a creature he was! Never have I felt such a horse between my knees. His great haunches gathered under him with every stride, and he shot forward ever faster and faster, stretched like a greyhound, while the wind beat in my face and whistled past my ears. I was wearing our undress jacket, a uniform simple and dark in itself – though some figures give distinction to any uniform – and I had taken the precaution to remove the long panache from my busby. The result was that, amidst the mixture of costumes in the hunt, there was no reason why mine should attract attention, or why these men, whose thoughts were all with the chase, should give any heed to me. The idea that a French officer might be riding with them was too absurd to enter their minds. I laughed as I rode, for, indeed, amid all the danger, there was something of comic in the situation.

I have said that the hunters were very unequally mounted, and so, at the end of a few miles, instead of being one body of men, like a charging regiment, they were scattered over a considerable space, the better riders well up to the dogs, and the others trailing away behind. Now, I was as good a rider as any, and my horse was the best of them all, and so you can imagine that it was not long before he carried me to the front. And when I saw the dogs streaming over the open, and the red-coated huntsmen behind them, and only seven or eight horsemen between us, then it was that the strangest thing of all happened, for I, too, went mad – I, Etienne Gerard! In a moment it came upon me, this spirit of sport, this desire to excel, this hatred of the fox. Accursed animal, should he then defy us ? Vile robber, his hour was come! Ah, it is a great feeling, this feeling of sport, my friends, this desire to trample the fox under the hoofs of your horse. I have made the fox-chase with the English. I have also, as I may tell you some day, fought the box-fight with the Bustler, of Bristol. And I say to you that this sport is a wonderful thing – full of interest as well as madness.

The farther we went the faster galloped my horse, and soon there were but three men as near the dogs as I was. All thought of fear of discovery had vanished. My brain throbbed, my blood ran hot – only one thing upon earth seemed worth living for, and that was to overtake this infernal fox. I passed one of the horsemen – a Hussar like myself. There were only two in front of me now – the one in a black coat, the other the blue artilleryman whom I had seen at the inn. His grey whiskers streamed in the wind, but he rode magnificently. For a mile or more we kept in this order, and then, as we galloped up a steep slope, my lighter weight brought me to the front. I passed them both, and when I reached the crown I was riding level with the little, hard-faced English huntsman. In front of us were the dogs, and then, a hundred paces beyond them, was a brown wisp of a thing, the fox itself, stretched to the uttermost. The sight of him fired my blood. 'Aha, we have you then, assassin!' I cried, and shouted my encouragement to the huntsman. I waved my hand to show him that there was one upon whom he could rely.

And now there were only the dogs between me and my prey. These dogs, whose duty it is to point out the game, were now rather a hindrance than a help to us, for it was hard to know how to pass them. The huntsman felt the difficulty as much as I, for he rode behind them and could make no progress towards the fox. He was a swift rider, but wanting in enterprise. For my part, I felt that it would be unworthy of the Hussars of Conflans if I could not overcome such a difficulty as this. Was Etienne Gerard to be stopped by a herd of fox-dogs? It was absurd. I gave a shout and spurred my horse.

'Hold hard, sir! Hold hard!' cried the huntsman.

He was uneasy for me, this good old man, but I reassured him by a wave and a smile. The dogs opened in front of me. One or two may have been hurt, but what would you have? The egg must be broken for the omelette. I could hear the huntsman shouting his congratulations behind me. One more effort, and the dogs were all behind me. Only the fox was in front.

Ah, the joy and pride of that moment! To know that I had beaten the English at their own sport. Here were three hundred all thirsting for the life of this animal, and yet it was I who was about to take it. I thought of my comrades of the light cavalry brigade, of my mother, of the Emperor, of France. I had brought honour to each and all. Every instant brought me nearer to the fox. The moment for action had arrived, so I unsheathed my sabre. I waved it in the air, and the brave English all shouted behind me.

Only then did I understand how difficult is this fox-chase, for one may cut again and again at the creature and never strike him once. He is small, and turns quickly from a blow. At every cut I heard those shouts of encouragement behind me, and they spurred me to yet another effort. And then at last the supreme moment of my triumph arrived. In the very act of turning I caught him fair with such another back-handed cut as that with which I killed the aide-de-camp of the Emperor of Russia. He flew into two pieces, his head one way and his tail another. I looked back and waved the blood-stained sabre in the air. For the moment I was exalted – superb!

Ah! how I should have loved to have waited to have received the congratulations of these generous enemies. There were fifty of them in sight, and not one of them who was not waving his hand and shouting. They are not really such a phlegmatic race, the English. A gallant deed in war or in sport will always warm their hearts. As to the old huntsman, he was the nearest to me, and I could see with my own eyes how overcome he was by what he had seen. He was like a man paralysed – his mouth open, his hand, with outspread fingers, raised in the air. For a moment my inclination was to return and embrace him. But already the call of duty was sounding in my ears, and these English, in spite of all the fraternity which exists among sportsmen, would certainly have made me prisoner. There was no hope for my mission now, and I had done all that I could do. I could see the lines of Massena's camp no very great distance off, for, by a lucky chance, the chase had taken us in that direction. I turned from the dead fox, saluted with my sabre, and galloped away.

But they would not leave me so easily, these gallant huntsmen. I was the fox now, and the chase swept bravely over the plain. It was only at the moment when I started for the camp that they could have known that I was a Frenchman, and now the whole swarm of them were at my heels. We were within gunshot of our pickets before they would halt, and then they stood in knots and would not go away, but shouted and waved their hands at me. No, I will not think that it was in enmity. Rather would I fancy that a glow of admiration filled their breasts, and that their one desire was to embrace the stranger who had carried himself so gallantly and well.

4 How the Brigadier saved an army

I have told you, my friends, how we held the English shut up for six months, from October, 1810, to March, 1811, within their lines of Torres Vedras. It was during this time that I hunted the fox in their company, and showed them that amidst all their sportsmen there was not one who could outride a Hussar of Conflans. When I galloped back into the French lines with the blood of the creature still moist upon my blade, the outposts who had seen what I had done raised a frenzied cry in my honour, whilst these English hunters still yelled behind me, so that I had the applause of both armies. It made the tears rise to my eyes to feel that I had won the admiration of so many brave men. These English are generous foes. That very evening there came a packet under a white flag addressed 'To the Hussar officer who cut down the fox.' Within I found the fox itself in two pieces, as I had left it. There was a note also, short but hearty as the English fashion is, to say that as I had slaughtered the fox it only remained for me to eat it. They could not know that it was not our French custom to eat foxes, and it showed their desire that he who had won the honours of the chase should also partake of the game. It is not for a Frenchman to be outdone in politeness, and so I returned it to these brave hunters, and begged them to accept it as a side-dish for their next *déjeuner de la chasse*. It is thus that chivalrous opponents make war.

I had brought back with me from my ride a clear plan of the English lines, and this I laid before Massena that very evening.

I had hoped that it would lead him to attack, but all the marshals were at each other's throats, snapping and growling like so many hungry hounds. Ney hated Massena, and Massena hated Junot, and Soult hated them all. For this reason nothing was done. In the meantime food grew more and more scarce, and our beautiful cavalry was ruined for want of fodder. With the end of the winter we had swept the whole country bare, and nothing remained for us to eat, although we sent our forage parties far and wide. It was clear even to the bravest of us that the time had come to retreat. I was myself forced to admit it.

But retreat was not so easy. Not only were the troops weak and exhausted from want of supplies, but the enemy had been much encouraged by our long inaction. Of Wellington we had no great fear. We had found him to be brave and cautious, but with little enterprise. Besides, in that barren country his pursuit could not be rapid. But on our flanks and in our rear there had gathered great numbers of Portuguese militia, of armed peasants, and of guerillas. These people had kept a safe distance all the winter, but now that our horses were foundered they were as thick as flies all round our outposts, and no man's life was worth a sou when once he fell into their hands. I could name a dozen officers of my own acquaintance who were cut off during that time, and the luckiest was he who received a ball from behind a rock through his head or his heart. There were some whose deaths were so terrible that no report of them was ever allowed to reach their relatives. So frequent were these tragedies, and so much did they impress the imagination of the men, that it became very difficult to induce them to leave the camp. There was one especial scoundrel, a guerilla chief named Manuelo, 'The Smiler', whose exploits filled our men with horror. He was a large, fat man of jovial aspect, and he lurked with a fierce gang among the mountains which lay upon our left flank. A volume might be written of this fellow's cruelties and brutalities, but he was certainly a man of power, for he organised his brigands in a manner which made it almost impossible for us to get through his country. This he did by imposing a severe discipline upon them and enforcing it by cruel penalties, a policy by which he made them formidable, but which had some unexpected results, as I will show you in my story. Had he not flogged his own lieutenant – but you will hear of that when the time comes.

There were many difficulties in connection with a retreat, but it was very evident that there was no other possible course, and so Massena began to quickly pass his baggage and his sick from Torres Novas, which was his head-quarters, to Coimbra, the first strong post on his line of communications. He could not do this unperceived, how-ever, and at once the guerillas came swarming closer and closer upon our flanks. One of our divisions, that of Clausel, with a brigade of Montbrun's cavalry, was far to the south of the Tagus, and it became very necessary to let them know that we were about to retreat, for otherwise they would be left unsupported in the very heart of the enemy's country. I remember wondering how Massena would accomplish this, for simple couriers could not get through, and small parties would be certainly destroyed. In some way an order to fall back must be conveyed to these men, or France would be the weaker by fourteen thousand men. Little did I think that it was I, Colonel Gerard, who was to have the honour of a deed which might have formed the crowning glory of any other man's life, and which stands high among those exploits which have made my own so famous.

At that time I was serving on Massena's staff, and he had two other aides-de-camp, who were also very brave and intelligent officers. The name of one was Cortex and of the other Duplessis. They were senior to me in age, but junior in every other respect. Cortex was a small, dark man, very quick and eager. He was a fine soldier, but he was ruined by his conceit. To take him at his own valuation, he was the first man in the army. Duplessis was a Gascon, like myself, and he was a very fine fellow, as all Gascon gentlemen are. We took it in turn, day about, to do duty, and it was Cortex who was in attendance upon the morning of which I speak. I saw him at breakfast, but afterwards neither he nor his horse was to be seen. All day Massena was in his usual gloom, and he spent much of his time staring with his telescope at the English lines and at the shipping in the Tagus. He said nothing of the mission upon which he had sent our comrade, and it was not for us to ask him any questions.

That night, about twelve o'clock, I was standing outside the Marshal's headquarters when he came out and stood motionless for half an hour, his arms folded upon his breast, staring through the darkness towards the east. So rigid and intent was he that you might have believed the muffled figure and the cocked hat to have been the statue of the man. What he was looking for I could not imagine; but at last he gave a bitter curse, and, turning on his heel, he went back into the house, banging the door behind him.

Next day the second aide-de-camp, Duplessis, had an interview with Massena in the morning, after which neither he nor his horse was seen again. That night, as I sat in the ante-room, the Marshal passed me, and I observed him through the window standing and staring to the east exactly as he had done before. For fully half an hour he remained there, a black shadow in the gloom. Then he strode in, the door banged, and I heard his spurs and his scabbard jingling and clanking through the passage. At the best he was a savage old man, but when he was crossed I had almost as soon face the Emperor himself. I heard him that night cursing and stamping above my head, but he did not send for me, and I knew him too well to go unsought.

Next morning it was my turn, for I was the only aide-de-camp left. I was his favourite aide-de-camp. His heart went out always to a smart soldier. I declare that I think there were tears in his black eyes when he sent for me that morning.

'Gerard!' said he. 'Come here!'

With a friendly gesture he took me by the sleeve and he led me to the open window which faced the east. Beneath us was the infantry camp, and beyond that the lines of the cavalry with the long rows of picketed horses. We could see the French outposts, and then a stretch of open country, intersected by vineyards. A range of hills lay beyond, with one well-marked peak towering above them. Round the base of these hills was a broad belt of forest. A single road ran white and clear, dipping and rising until it passed through a gap in the hills.

'This,' said Massena, pointing to the mountain, 'is the Sierra de Merodal. Do you perceive anything upon the top?'

I answered that I did not.

'Now?' he asked, and he handed me his field-glass.

With its aid I perceived a small mound or cairn upon the crest.

'What you see,' said the Marshal, 'is a pile of logs which was placed there as a beacon. We laid it when the country was in our hands, and now, although we no longer hold it, the beacon remains undisturbed. Gerard, that beacon must be lit tonight. France needs it, the Emperor needs it, the army needs it. Two of your comrades have gone to light it, but neither has made his way to the summit. Today it is your turn, and I pray that you may have better luck.'

It is not for a soldier to ask the reason for his orders, and so I was about to hurry from the room, but the Marshal laid his hand upon my shoulder and held me.

'You shall know all, and so learn how high is the cause for which you risk your life,' said he. 'Fifty miles to the south of us, on the other side of the Tagus, is the army of General Clausel. His camp is situated near a peak named the Sierra d'Ossa. On the summit of this peak is a beacon, and by this beacon he has a picket. It is agreed between us that when at midnight he shall see our signal fire he shall light his own as an answer, and shall then at once fall back upon the main army. If he does not start at once I must go without him. For two days I have endeavoured to send him his message. It must reach him today, or his army will be left behind and destroyed.'

Ah, my friends, how my heart swelled when I heard how high was the task which Fortune had assigned to me! If my life were spared, here was one more splendid new leaf for my laurel crown. If, on the other hand, I died, then it would be a death worthy of such a career. I said nothing, but I cannot doubt that all the noble thoughts that were in me shone in my face, for Massena took my hand and wrung it.

'There is the hill and there the beacon,' said he. 'There is only this guerilla and his men between you and it. I cannot detach a large party for the enterprise, and a small one would be seen and destroyed. Therefore to you alone I commit it. Carry it out in your own way, but at twelve o'clock this night let me see the fire upon the hill.'

'If it is not there,' said I, 'then I pray you, Marshal Massena, to see that my effects are sold and the money sent to my mother.' So I raised my hand to my busby and turned upon my heel, my heart glowing at the thought of the great exploit which lay before me.

I sat in my own chamber for some little time considering how I had best take the matter in hand. The fact that neither Cortex nor Duplessis, who were very zealous and active officers, had succeeded in reaching the summit of the Sierra de Merodal showed that the country was very closely watched by the guerillas. I reckoned out the distance upon a map. There were ten miles of open country to be crossed before reaching the hills. Then came a belt of forest on the lower slopes of the mountain, which may have been three or four miles wide. And then there was the actual peak itself, of no very great height, but without any cover to conceal me. Those were the three stages of my journey.

It seemed to me that once I had reached the shelter of the wood all would be easy, for I could lie concealed within its shadows and climb upwards under the cover of night. From eight till twelve would give me four hours of darkness in which to make the ascent. It was only the first stage, then, which I had seriously to consider.

Over that flat country there lay the inviting white road, and I remembered that my comrades had both taken their horses. That was clearly their ruin, for nothing could be easier than for the brigands to keep watch upon the road, and to lay an ambush for all who passed along it. It would not be difficult for me to ride across country, and I was well horsed at that time, for I had not only Violette and Rataplan, who were two of the finest mounts in the army, but I had the splendid black English hunter which I had taken from Sir Cotton. However, after much thought, I determined to go upon foot, since I should then be in a better state to take advantage of any chance which might offer. As to my dress, I covered my Hussar uniform with a long cloak, and I put a grey forage cap upon my head. You may ask me why I did not dress as a peasant, but I answer that a man of honour has no desire to die the death of a spy. It is one thing to be murdered, and it is another to be justly executed by the laws of war. I would not run the risk of such an end.

In the late afternoon I stole out of the camp and passed through the line of our pickets. Beneath my cloak I had a field-glass and a pocket pistol, as well as my sword. In my pocket were tinder, flint, and steel.

For two or three miles I kept under cover of the vine-yards, and made such good progress that my heart was high within me, and I thought to myself that it only needed a man of some brains to take the matter in hand to bring it easily to success. Of course, Cortex and Duplessis galloping down the high road would be easily seen, but the intelligent Gerard lurking among the vines was quite another person. I dare say I had got as far as five miles before I met any check. At that point there is a small winehouse, round which I perceived some carts and a number of people, the first that I had seen. Now that I was well outside the lines I knew that every person was my enemy, so I crouched lower while I stole along to a point from which I could get a better view of what was going on. I then perceived that these people were peasants, who were loading two waggons with empty wine-casks. I failed to see how they could either help or hinder me, so I continued upon my way.

But soon I understood that my task was not so simple as had appeared. As the ground rose the vineyards ceased, and I came upon a stretch of open country studded with low hills. Crouching in a ditch I examined them with a glass, and I very soon perceived that there was a watcher upon every one of them, and that these people had a line of pickets and outposts thrown forward exactly like our own. I had heard of the discipline which was practised by this scoundrel whom they called 'The Smiler', and this, no doubt, was an example of it. Between the hills there was a cordon of sentries, and, though I worked some distance round to the flank, I still found myself faced by the enemy. It was a puzzle what to do. There was so little cover that a rat could hardly cross without being seen. Of course, it would be easy enough to slip through at night, as I had done with the English at Torres Vedras; but I was still far from the mountain, and I could not in that case reach it in time to light the midnight beacon. I lay in my ditch and I made a thousand plans, each more dangerous than the last. And then suddenly I had that flash of light which comes to the brave man who refuses to despair.

You remember I have mentioned that two waggons were loading up with empty casks at the inn. The heads of the oxen were turned to the east, and it was evident that those waggons were going in the direction which I desired. Could I only conceal myself upon one of them, what better and easier way could I find of passing through the lines of the guerillas? So simple and so good was the plan that I could not restrain a cry of delight as it crossed my mind, and I hurried away instantly in the direction of the inn. There, from behind some bushes, I had a good look at what was going on upon the road.

There were three peasants with red montero caps loading the barrels, and they had completed one waggon and the lower tier of the other. A number of empty barrels still lay outside the winehouse waiting to be put on. Fortune was my friend – I have always said that she is a woman and cannot resist a dashing young Hussar. As I watched, the three fellows went into the inn, for the day was hot, and they were thirsty after their labour. Quick as a flash I darted out from my hiding-place, climbed on to the waggon, and crept into one of the empty casks. It had a bottom but no top, and it lay upon its side with the open end inwards.

There I crouched like a dog in its kennel, my knees drawn up to my chin; for the barrels were not very large and I am a well-grown man. As I lay there out came the three peasants again, and presently I heard a crash upon the top of me, which told that I had another barrel above me. They piled them upon the cart until I could not imagine how I was ever to get out again. However, it is time to think of crossing the Vistula when you are over the Rhine, and I had no doubt that if chance and my own wits had carried me so far they would carry me farther.

Soon, when the waggon was full, they set forth upon their way, and I within my barrel chuckled at every step, for it was carrying me whither I wished to go. We travelled slowly, and the peasants walked beside the waggons. This I knew, because I heard their voices close to me. They seemed to me to be very merry fellows, for they laughed heartily as they went. What the joke was I could not understand. Though I speak their language fairly well I could not hear anything comic in the scraps of their conversation which met my ear.

I reckoned that at the rate of walking of a team of oxen we covered about two miles an hour. Therefore, when I was sure that two and a half hours had passed – such hours, my friends, cramped, suffocated, and nearly poisoned with the fumes of the lees – when they had passed, I was sure that the dangerous open country was behind us, and that we were upon the edge of the forest and the mountain. So now I had to turn my mind upon how I was to get out of my barrel. I had thought of several ways, and was balancing one against the other, when the question was decided for me in a very simple but unexpected manner.

The waggon stopped suddenly with a jerk, and I heard a number of gruff voices in excited talk. 'Where, where?' cried one. 'On our cart,' said another. 'Who is he?' said a third. 'A French officer; I saw his cap and his boots.' They all roared with laughter. 'I was looking out of the window of the *posada* and I saw him spring into the cask like a toreador with a Seville bull at his heels.' 'Which cask, then?'

'It was this one,' said the fellow, and, sure enough, his fist struck the wood beside my head.

What a situation, my friends, for a man of my standing! I blush now, after forty years, when I think of it. To be trussed like a fowl and to listen helplessly to the rude laughter of these boors – to know, too, that my mission had come to an ignominious and even ridiculous end. I would have blessed the man who would have sent a bullet through the cask and freed me from my misery.

I heard the crashing of the barrels as they hurled them off the waggon, and then a couple of bearded faces and the muzzles of two guns looked in at me. They seized me by the sleeves of my coat, and they dragged me out into the daylight. A strange figure I must have looked as I stood blinking and gaping in the blinding sunlight. My body was bent like a cripple's, for I could not straighten my stiff joints, and half my coat was as red as an English soldier's from the lees in which I had lain. They laughed and laughed, these dogs, and as I tried to express by my bearing and gestures the contempt in which I held them, their laughter grew all the louder. But even in these hard circumstances I bore myself like the man I am, and as I cast my eye slowly round I did not find that any of the laughers were very ready to face it.

That one glance round was enough to tell me exactly how I was situated. I had been betrayed by these peasants into the hands of an outpost of guerillas. There were eight of them, savage-looking, hairy creatures, with cotton handkerchiefs under their sombreros, and many-buttoned jackets with coloured sashes round the waist. Each had a gun and one or two pistols stuck in his girdle. The leader, a great bearded ruffian, held his gun against my ear while the others searched my pockets, taking from me my overcoat, my pistol, my glass, my sword, and, worst of all, my flint and steel and tinder. Come what might I was ruined, for I had no longer the means of lighting the beacon even if I should reach it.

Eight of them, my friends, with three peasants, and I unarmed! Was Etienne Gerard in despair? Did he lose his wits? Ah, you know me too well; but they did not know me yet, these dogs of brigands. Never have I made so supreme and astounding an effort as at this very instant when all seemed lost. Yet you might guess many times before you would hit upon the device by which I escaped them. Listen and I will tell you.

They had dragged me from the waggon when they searched me, and I stood, still twisted and warped, in the midst of them. But the stiffness was wearing off, and already my mind was very actively looking out for some method of breaking away. It was a narrow pass in which the brigands had their outpost. It was bounded on the one hand by a steep mountain side. On the other the ground fell away in a very long slope, which ended in a bushy valley many hundreds of feet below. These fellows, you understand, were hardy mountaineers, who could travel either up hill or down very much quicker than I. They wore *abarcas*, or shoes of skin, tied on like sandals, which gave them a foothold everywhere. A less resolute man would have despaired. But in an instant I saw and used the strange chance which Fortune had placed in my way. On the very edge of the slope was one of the wine-barrels. I moved slowly towards it, and then with a tiger spring I dived into it feet foremost, and with a roll of my body I tipped it over the side of the hill.

Shall I ever forget that dreadful journey – how I bounded and crashed and whizzed down that terrible slope? I had dug in my knees and elbows, bunching my body into a compact bundle so as to steady it; but my head projected from the end, and it was a marvel that I did not dash out my brains. There were long, smooth slopes and then came steeper scarps where the barrel ceased to roll, and sprang into the air like a goat, coming down with a rattle and crash which jarred every bone in my body. How the wind whistled in my ears, and my head turned and turned until I was sick and giddy and nearly senseless! Then, with a swish and a great rasping and crackling of branches, I reached the bushes which I had seen so far below me. Through them I broke my way, down a slope beyond, and deep into another patch of underwood, where striking a sapling my barrel flew to pieces. From amid a heap of staves and hoops I crawled out, my body aching in every inch of it, but my heart singing loudly with joy and my spirit high within me, for I knew how great was the feat which I had accomplished, and I already seemed to see the beacon blazing on the hill.

A horrible nausea had seized me from the tossing which I had undergone, and I felt as I did upon the ocean when first I experienced those movements of which the English have taken so perfidious an advantage. I had to sit for a few moments with my head upon my hands beside the ruins of my barrel. But there was no time for rest. Already I heard shouts above me which told that my pursuers were descending the hill. I dashed into the thickest part of the underwood, and I ran and ran until I was utterly exhausted. Then I lay panting and listened with all my ears, but no sound came to them. I had shaken off my enemies.

When I had recovered my breath I travelled swiftly on, and waded knee-deep through several brooks, for it came into my head that they might follow me with dogs. On gaining a clear place and looking round me, I found to my delight that in spite of my adventures I had not been much out of my way. Above me towered the peak of Merodal, with its bare and bold summit shooting out of the groves of dwarf oaks which shrouded its flanks. These groves were the continuation of the cover under which I found myself, and it seemed to me that I had nothing to fear now until I reached the other side of the forest. At the same time I knew that every man's hand was against me, that I was unarmed, and that there were many people about me. I saw no one, but several times I heard shrill whistles, and once the sound of a gun in the distance.

It was hard work pushing one's way through the bushes, and so I was glad when I came to the larger trees and found a path which led between them. Of course, I was too wise to walk upon it, but I kept near it and followed its course. I had gone some distance, and had, as I imagined, nearly reached the limit of the wood, when a strange, moaning sound fell upon my ears. At first I thought it was the cry of some animal, but then there came words, of which I only caught the French exclamation, 'Mon Dieu!' With great caution I advanced in the direction from which the sound proceeded, and this is what I saw.

On a couch of dried leaves there was stretched a man dressed in the same grey uniform which I wore myself. He was evidently horribly wounded, for he held a cloth to his breast which was crimson with his blood. A pool had formed all round his couch, and he lay in a haze of flies, whose buzzing and droning would certainly have called my attention if his groans had not come to my ear. I lay for a moment, fearing some trap, and then, my pity and loyalty rising above all other feelings, I ran forward and knelt by his side. He turned a haggard face upon me, and it was Duplessis, the man who had gone before me. It needed but one glance at his sunken cheeks and glazing eyes to tell me that he was dying.

'Gerard!' said he; 'Gerard!'

I could but look my sympathy, but he, though the life was ebbing swiftly out of him, still kept his duty before him, like the gallant gentleman he was.

'The beacon, Gerard! You will light it?'

'Have you flint and steel?'

'It is here.'

'Then I will light it tonight.'

'I die happy to hear you say so. They shot me, Gerard. But you will tell the Marshal that I did my best.'

'And Cortex?'

'He was less fortunate. He fell into their hands and died horribly. If you see that you cannot get away, Gerard, put a bullet into your own heart. Don't die as Cortex did.'

I could see that his breath was failing, and I bent low to catch his words.

'Can you tell me anything which can help me in my task?' I asked.

'Yes, yes; De Pombal. He will help you. Trust De Pombal.' With the words his head fell back and he was dead.

'Trust De Pombal. It is good advice.' To my amazement a man was standing at the very side of me. So absorbed had I been in my comrade's words and intent on his advice that he had crept up without my observing him. Now I sprang to my feet and faced him. He was a tall, dark fellow, black-haired, black-eyed, black-bearded, with a long, sad face. In his hand he had a wine-bottle and over his shoulder was slung one of the *trebucos*, or blunderbusses, which these fellows bear. He made no effort to unsling it, and I understood that this was the man to whom my dead friend had commended me.

'Alas, he is gone!' said he, bending over Duplessis. 'He fled into the wood after he was shot, but I was fortunate enough to find where he had fallen and to make his last hours more easy. This couch was my making, and I had brought this wine to slake his thirst.'

'Sir,' said I, 'in the name of France I thank you. I am but a colonel of light cavalry, but I am Etienne Gerard, and the name stands for something in the French army. May I ask—'

'Yes, sir, I am Aloysius de Pombal, younger brother of the famous nobleman of that name. At present I am the first lieutenant in the band of the guerilla chief who is usually known as Manuelo, "The Smiler".'

My word, I clapped my hand to the place where my pistol should have been, but the man only smiled at the gesture.

'I am his first lieutenant, but I am also his deadly enemy,' said he. He slipped off his jacket and pulled up his shirt as he spoke. 'Look at this!' he cried, and he turned upon me a back which was all scored and lacerated with red and purple weals. 'This is what "The Smiler" has done to me, a man with the noblest blood of Portugal in my veins. What I will do to "The Smiler" you have still to see.'

There was such fury in his eyes and in the grin of his white teeth that I could no longer doubt his truth, with that clotted and oozing back to corroborate his words.

'I have ten men sworn to stand by me,' said he. 'In a few

days I hope to join your army, when I have done my work here. In the meanwhile—' A strange change came over his face, and he suddenly slung his musket to the front: 'Hold up your hands, you French hound!' he yelled. 'Up with them, or I blow your head off!'

You start, my friends! You stare! Think, then, how I stared and started at this sudden ending of our talk. There was the black muzzle, and there the dark, angry eyes behind it. What could I do? I was helpless. I raised my hands in the air. At the same moment voices sounded from all parts of the wood, there were crying and calling and rushing of many feet. A swarm of dreadful figures broke through the green bushes, a dozen hands seized me, and I, poor, luckless, frenzied I, was a prisoner once more. Thank God, there was no pistol which I could have plucked from my belt and snapped at my own head. Had I been armed at that moment I should not be sitting here in this café and telling you these old-world tales.

With grimy, hairy hands clutching me on every side I was led along the pathway through the wood, the villain De Pombal giving directions to my captors. Four of the brigands carried up the dead body of Duplessis. The shadows of evening were already falling when we cleared the forest and came out upon the mountain-side. Up this I was driven until we reached the headquarters of the guerillas, which lay in a cleft close to the summit of the mountain. There was the beacon which had cost me so much, a square stack of wood, immediately above our heads. Below were two or three huts which had belonged, no doubt, to goatherds, and which were now used to shelter these rascals. Into one of these I was cast, bound and help-less, and the dead body of my poor comrade was laid beside me.

I was lying there with the one thought still consuming me, how to wait a few hours and to get at that pile of faggots above my head, when the door of my prison opened and a man entered. Had my hands been free I should have flown at his throat, for it was none other than De Pombal. A couple of brigands were at his heels, but he ordered them back and closed the door behind him.

'You villain!' said I.

'Hush!' he cried. 'Speak low, for I do not know who may be listening, and my life is at stake. I have some words to say to you, Colonel Gerard; I wish well to you, as I did to your dead companion. As I spoke to you beside his body I saw that we were surrounded, and that your capture was unavoidable. I should have shared your fate had I hesitated. I instantly captured you myself, so as to preserve the confidence of the band. Your own sense will tell you that there was nothing else for me to do. I do not know now whether I can save you, but at least I will try.'

This was a new light upon the situation. I told him that I could not tell how far he spoke the truth, but that I would judge him by his actions.

'I ask nothing better,' said he. 'A word of advice to you! The chief will see you now. Speak him fair, or he will have you sawn between two planks. Contradict nothing he says. Give him such information he wants. It is your only chance. If you can gain time something may come in our favour. Now, I have no more time. Come at once, or suspicion may be awakened.' He helped me to rise and then, opening the door, he dragged me out very roughly, and with the aid of the fellows outside he brutally pushed and thrust me to the place where the guerilla chief was seated, with his rude followers gathered round him.

A remarkable man was Manuelo, 'The Smiler'. He was fat and florid and comfortable, with a big, clean-shaven face and a bald head, the very model of a kindly father of a family. As I looked at his honest smile I could scarcely believe that this was, indeed, the infamous ruffian whose name was a horror through the English Army as well as our own. It is well known that Trent, who was a British officer, afterwards had the fellow hanged for his brutalities. He sat upon a boulder and he beamed upon me like one who meets an old acquaintance. I observed, however, that one of his men leaned upon a long saw, and the sight was enough to cure me of all delusions.

'Good evening, Colonel Gerard,' said he. 'We have been highly honoured by General Massena's staff: Major Cortex one day, Colonel Duplessis the next, and now Colonel Gerard. Possibly the Marshal himself may be induced to honour us with a visit. You have seen Duplessis, I understand. Cortex you will find nailed to a tree down yonder. It only remains to be decided how we can best dispose of yourself.'

It was not a cheering speech; but all the time his fat face was wreathed in smiles, and he lisped out his words in the most mincing and amiable fashion. Now, however, he suddenly leaned forward, and I read a very real intensity in his eyes.

'Colonel Gerard,' said he, 'I cannot promise you your life, for it is not our custom, but I can give you an easy death or I can give you a terrible one. Which shall it be?'

'What do you wish me to do in exchange?'

'If you would die easy I ask you to give me truthful answers to the questions which I ask.'

A sudden thought flashed through my mind.

'You wish to kill me,' said I; 'it cannot matter to you how I die. If I answer your questions, will you let me choose the manner of my own death?'

'Yes, I will,' said he, 'so long as it is before midnight tonight.'

'Swear it!' I cried.

'The word of a Portuguese gentleman is sufficient,' said he.

'Not a word will I say until you have sworn it.'

He flushed with anger and his eyes swept round towards the saw. But he understood from my tone that I meant what I said, and that I was not a man to be bullied into submission. He pulled a cross from under his *zammara* or jacket of black sheepskin.

'I swear it,' said he.

Oh, my joy as I heard the words! What an end – what an end for the first swordsman of France! I could have laughed with delight at the thought.

'Now, your questions!' said I.

'You swear in turn to answer them truly?'

'I do, upon the honour of a gentleman and a soldier.' It was, as you perceive, a terrible thing that I promised, but what was it compared to what I might gain by compliance?

'This is a very fair and interesting bargain,' said he, taking a note-book from his pocket. 'Would you kindly turn your gaze towards the French camp?'

Following the direction of his gesture, I turned and looked down upon the camp in the plain beneath us. In spite of the fifteen miles, one could in that clear atmosphere see every detail with the utmost distinctness. There were the long squares of our tents and our huts, with the cavalry lines and the dark patches which marked the ten batteries of artillery. How sad to think of my magnificent regiment waiting down yonder, and to know that they would never see their colonel again! With one squadron of them I could have swept all these cut-throats off the face of the earth. My eager eyes filled with tears as I looked at the corner of the camp where I knew that there were eight hundred men, any one of whom would have died for his colonel. But my sadness vanished when I saw behind the tents the plumes of smoke which marked the headquarters at Torres Novas. There was Massena, and, please God, at the cost of my life his mission would that night be done. A spasm of pride and exultation filled my breast. I should have liked to have had a voice of thunder that I might call to them, 'Behold it is I, Etienne Gerard, who will die in order to save the army of Clausel!' It was, indeed, sad to think that so noble a deed should be done, and that no one should be there to tell the tale.

'Now,' said the brigand chief, 'you see the camp and you see also the road which leads to Coimbra. It is crowded with your fourgons and your ambulances. Does this mean that Massena is about to retreat?'

One could see the dark moving lines of waggons with an occasional flash of steel from the escort. There could, apart from my promise, be no indiscretion in admitting that which was already obvious.

'He will retreat,' said I.

'By Coimbra?'

'I believe so.'

'But the army of Clausel?'

I shrugged my shoulders.

'Every path to the south is blocked. No message can reach them. If Massena falls back the army of Clausel is doomed.'

'It must take its chance,' said I.

'How many men has he?'

'I should say about fourteen thousand.'

'How much cavalry?'

'One brigade of Montbrun's Division.'

'What regiments?'

'The 4th Chasseurs, the 9th Hussars, and a regiment of Cuirassiers.'

'Quite right,' said he, looking at his note-book. 'I can tell you speak the truth, and Heaven help you if you don't.' Then, division by division, he went over the whole army, asking the composition of each brigade. Need I tell you that I would have had my tongue torn out before I would have told him such things had I not a greater end in view? I would let him know all if I could but save the army of Clausel.

At last he closed his note-book and replaced it in his pocket. 'I am obliged to you for this information, which shall reach Lord Wellington tomorrow,' said he. 'You have done your share of the bargain; it is for me now to perform mine. How would you wish to die? As a soldier you would, no doubt, prefer to be shot, but some think that a jump over the Merodal precipice is really an easier death. A good few have taken it, but we were, unfortunately, never able to get an opinion from them afterwards. There is the saw, too, which does not appear to be popular. We could hang you, no doubt, but it would involve the inconvenience of going down to the wood. However, a promise is a promise, and you seem to be an excellent fellow, so we will spare no pains to meet your wishes.'

'You said,' I answered, 'that I must die before midnight. I will choose, therefore, just one minute before that hour.'

'Very good,' said he. 'Such clinging to life is rather childish, but your wishes shall be met.'

'As to the method,' I added, 'I love a death which all the world can see. Put me on yonder pile of faggots and burn me alive, as saints and martyrs have been burned before me. That is no common end, but one which an Emperor might envy.'

The idea seemed to amuse him very much.

'Why not?' said he. 'If Massena has sent you to spy upon us, he may guess what the fire upon the mountains means.'

'Exactly,' said I. 'You have hit upon my very reason. He will guess, and all will know, that I have died a soldier's death.'

'I see no objection whatever,' said the brigand, with his abominable smile. 'I will send some goat's flesh and wine into your hut. The sun is sinking, and it is nearly eight o'clock. In four hours be ready for your end.'

It was a beautiful world to be leaving. I looked at the golden haze below, where the last rays of the sinking sun shone upon the blue waters of the winding Tagus and gleamed upon the white sails of the English transports. Very beautiful it was, and very sad to leave; but there are things more beautiful than that. The death that is died for the sake of others, honour, and duty, and loyalty, and love – these are the beauties far brighter than any which the eye can see. My breast was filled with admiration for my own most noble conduct, and with wonder whether any soul would ever come to know how I had placed myself in the heart of the beacon which saved the army of Clausel. I hoped so and I prayed so, for what a consolation it would be to my mother, what an example to the army, what a pride to my Hussars! When De Pombal came at last into my hut with the food and wine, the first request I made him was that he would write an account of my death and send it to the French camp. He answered not a word, but I ate my supper with a better appetite from the thought that my glorious fate would not be altogether unknown.

I had been there about two hours when the door opened again, and the chief stood looking in. I was in darkness, but a brigand with a torch stood beside him, and I saw his eyes and his teeth gleaming as he peered at me.

'Ready?' he asked.

'It is not yet time.'

'You stand out for the last minute?'

'A promise is a promise.'

'Very good. Be it so. We have a little justice to do among ourselves, for one of my fellows has been misbehaving. We have a strict rule of our own which is no respecter of persons, as De Pombal here could tell you. Do you truss him and lay him on the faggots, De Pombal, and I will return to see him die.'

De Pombal and the man with the torch entered, while I heard the steps of the chief passing away. De Pombal closed the door.

'Colonel Gerard,' said he, 'you must trust this man, for he is one of my party. It is neck or nothing. We may save you yet. But I take a great risk, and I want a definite promise. If we save you, will you guarantee that we have a friendly reception in the French camp and that all the past will be forgotten?'

'I do guarantee it.'

'And I trust your honour. Now, quick, quick, there is not an instant to lose! If this monster returns we shall die horribly, all three.'

I stared in amazement at what he did. Catching up a long rope he wound it round the body of my dead comrade, and he tied a cloth round his mouth so as to almost cover his face.

'Do you lie there!' he cried, and he laid me in the place of the dead body. 'I have four of my men waiting, and they will place this upon the beacon.' He opened the door and gave an order. Several of the brigands entered and bore out Duplessis. For myself I remained upon the floor, with my mind in a turmoil of hope and wonder.

Five minutes later De Pombal and his men were back.

'You are laid upon the beacon,' said he; 'I defy anyone in the world to say it is not you, and you are so gagged and bound that no one can expect you to speak or move. Now, it only remains to carry forth the body of Duplessis and to toss it over the Merodal precipice.'

Two of them seized me by the head and two by the heels and carried me, stiff and inert, from the hut. As I came into the open air I could have cried out in my amazement. The moon had risen above the beacon, and there, clear outlined against its silver light, was the figure of the man stretched upon the top. The brigands were either in their camp or standing round the beacon, for none of them stopped or questioned our little party. De Pombal led them in the direction of the precipice. At the brow we were out of sight, and there I was allowed to use my feet once more. De Pombal pointed to a narrow, winding track.

'This is the way down,' said he, and then, suddenly, '*Dios mio*, what is that?'

A terrible cry had risen out of the woods beneath us. I saw that De Pombal was shivering like a frightened horse.

'It is that devil,' he whispered. 'He is treating another as he treated me. But on, on, for Heaven help us if he lays his hands upon us!'

One by one we crawled down the narrow goat-track. At the bottom of the cliff we were back in the woods once more. Suddenly a yellow glare shone above us, and the black shadows of the tree-trunks started out in front. They had fired the beacon behind us. Even from where we stood we could see that impassive body amid the flames, and the black figures of the guerillas as they danced, howling like cannibals, round the pile. Ha! how I shook my fist at them, the dogs, and how I vowed that one day my Hussars and I would make the reckoning level!

De Pombal knew how the outposts were placed and all the paths which led through the forest. But to avoid these villains we had to plunge among the hills and walk for many a weary mile. And yet how gladly would I have walked those extra leagues if only for one sight which they brought to my eyes! It may have been two o'clock in the morning when we halted upon the bare shoulder of a hill over which our path curled. Looking back we saw the red glow of the embers of the beacon as if volcanic fires were bursting from the tall peak of Merodal. And then, as I gazed, I saw something else – something which caused me to shriek with joy and to fall upon the ground, rolling in my delight. For, far away upon the southern horizon, there winked and twinkled one great yellow light, throbbing and flaming, the light of no house, the light of no star, but the answering beacon of Mount d'Ossa, which told that the army of Clausel knew what Etienne Gerard had been sent out to tell them.

5 How the Brigadier triumphed in England

I have told you, my friends, how I triumphed over the English at the fox-hunt when I pursued the animal so fiercely that even the herd of trained dogs was unable to keep up, and alone with my own hand I put him to the sword. Perhaps I have said too much of the matter, but there is a thrill in the triumphs of sport which even warfare cannot give, for in warfare you share your successes with your regiment and your army, but in sport it is you yourself unaided who have won the laurels. It is an advantage which the English have over us that in all classes they take great interest in every form of sport. It may be that they are richer than we, or it may be that they are more idle; but I was surprised when I was a prisoner in that country to observe how widespread was this feeling, and how much it filled the minds and the lives of the people. A horse that will run, a cock that will fight, a dog that will kill rats, a man that will box – they would turn away from the Emperor in all his glory in order to look upon any of these.

I could tell you many stories of English sport, for I saw much of it during the time that I was the guest of Lord Rufton, after the order for my exchange had come to England. There were months before I could be sent back to France, and during that time I stayed with this good Lord Rufton at his beautiful house at High Combe, which is at the northern end of Dartmoor. He had ridden with the police when they had pursued me from Princetown, and he had felt towards me when I was overtaken as I would myself have felt had I, in my own country, seen a brave and debonair soldier without a friend to help him. In a word, he took me to his house, clad me, fed me, and treated me as if he had been my brother. I will say this of the English, that they were always generous enemies, and very good people with whom to fight. In the Peninsula the Spanish outposts would present their muskets at ours, but the British their brandy flasks. And of all these generous men there was none who was the equal of this admirable milord, who held out so warm a hand to an enemy in distress.

Ah! what thoughts of sport it brings back to me, the very name of High Combe! I can see it now, the long, low, brick house, warm and ruddy, with white plaster pillars before the door. He was a great sportsman this Lord Rufton, and all who were about him were of the same sort. But you will be pleased to hear that there were few things in which I could not hold my own, and in some I excelled. Behind the house was a wood in which pheasants were reared, and it was Lord Rufton's joy to kill these birds, which was done by sending in men to drive them out while he and his friends stood outside and shot them as they passed. For my part I was more crafty, for I studied the habits of the birds, and stealing out in the evening I was able to kill a number of them as they roosted in the trees. Hardly a single shot was wasted, but the keeper was attracted by the sound of the firing, and he implored me in his rough English fashion to spare those that were left. That night I was able to place twelve birds as a surprise upon Lord Rufton's supper table, and he laughed until he cried, so overjoyed was he to see them. 'Gad, Gerard, you'll be the death of me yet!' he cried. Often he said the same thing, for at every turn I amazed him by the way in which I entered into the sports of the English.

There is a game called cricket which they play in the summer, and this also I learned. Rudd, the head gardener, was a famous player of cricket, and so was Lord Rufton himself. Before the house was a lawn, and here it was that Rudd taught me the game. It is a brave pastime, a game for soldiers, for each tries to strike the other with the ball, and it is but a small stick with which you may ward it off. Three sticks behind show the spot beyond which you may not retreat. I can tell you that it is no game for children, and I will confess that, in spite of my nine campaigns, I felt myself turn pale when first the ball flashed past me. So swift was it that I had not time to raise my stick to ward it off, but by good fortune it missed me and knocked down the wooden pins which marked the boundary. It was for Rudd then to defend himself and for me to attack. When I was a boy in Gascony I learned to throw both far and straight, so that I made sure that I could hit this gallant Englishman. With a shout I rushed forward and hurled the ball at him. It flew as swift as a bullet towards his ribs, but without a word he swung his staff and the ball rose a surprising distance in the air. Lord Rufton clapped his hands and cheered. Again the ball was brought to me, and again it was for me to throw. This time it flew past his head, and it seemed to me that it was his turn to look pale. But he was a brave man this gardener, and again he faced me. Ah, my friends, the hour of my triumph had come! It was a red waistcoat that he wore, and at this I hurled the ball. You would have said that I was a gunner, not a hussar, for never was so straight an aim. With a despairing cry – the cry of the brave man who is beaten – he fell upon the wooden pegs behind him, and they all rolled upon the ground together. He was cruel, this English milord, and he laughed so that he could not come to the aid of his servant. It was for me, the victor, to rush forwards to embrace this intrepid player, and to raise him to his feet with words of praise, and encouragement, and hope. He was in pain and could not stand erect, yet the honest fellow confessed that there was no accident in my victory. 'He did it a-purpose! He did it a-purpose!' Again and again he said it. Yes, it is a great game this cricket, and I would gladly have ventured upon it again but Lord Rufton and Rudd said that it was late in the season, and so they would play no more.

How foolish of me, the old broken man, to dwell upon these successes, and yet I will confess that my age has been very much soothed and comforted by the memory of the women who have loved me and the men whom I have overcome. It is pleasant to think that five years afterwards, when Lord Rufton came to Paris after the peace, he was able to assure me that my name was still a famous one in the north of Devonshire for the fine exploits that I had performed. Especially, he said, that they still talked over my boxing match with the Honourable Baldock. It came about in this way. Of an evening many sportsmen would assemble at the house of Lord Rufton, where they would drink much wine, make wild bets, and talk of their horses and their foxes. How well I remember those strange creatures. Sir Barrington, Jack Lupton of Barnstaple, Colonel Addison, Johnny Miller, Lord Sadler, and my enemy, the Honourable Baldock. They were of the same stamp all of them, drinkers, madcaps, fighters, gamblers, full of strange caprices and extraordinary whims. Yet they were kindly fellows in their rough fashion, save only this Baldock, a fat man who prided himself on his skill at the box-fight. It was he who, by his laughter against the French because they were ignorant of sport, caused me to challenge him in the very sport at which he excelled. You will say that it was foolish, my friends, but the decanter had passed many times, and the blood of youth ran hot in my veins. I would fight him, this boaster; I would show him that if we had not skill, at least we had courage. Lord Rufton would not allow it. I insisted. The others cheered me on and slapped me on the back. 'No, dash it, Baldock, he's our guest,' said Rufton. 'It's his own doing,' the other answered. 'Look here, Rufton, they can't hurt each other if they wear the mawleys,' cried Lord Sadler. And so it was agreed.

What the mawleys were I did not know; but presently they brought out four great puddings of leather, not unlike a fencing-glove, but larger. With these our hands were covered after we had stripped ourselves of our coats and our waistcoats. Then the table, with the glasses and decanters, was pushed into the corner of the room, and behold us, face to face! Lord Sadler sat in the armchair with a watch in his open hand. 'Time!' said he.

I will confess to you, my friends, that I felt at that moment a tremor such as none of my many duels have ever given me. With sword or pistol I am at home; but here I only understood that I must struggle with this fat Englishman and do what I could, in spite of these great puddings upon my hands, to overcome him. And at the very outset I was disarmed of the best weapon that was left to me. 'Mind, Gerard, no kicking!' said Lord Rufton in my ear. I had only a pair of thin dancing slippers, and yet the man was fat, and a few well-directed kicks might have left me the victor. But there is an etiquette just as there is in fencing, and I refrained. I looked at this Englishman and I wondered how I should attack him. His ears were large and prominent. Could I seize them I might drag him to the ground. I rushed in, but I was betrayed by this flabby glove, and twice I lost my hold. He struck me, but I cared little for his blows, and again I seized him by the ear. He fell, and I rolled upon him and thumped his head upon the ground. How they cheered and laughed, these gallant Englishmen, and how they clapped me on the back!

'Even money on the Frenchman,' cried Lord Sadler.

'He fights foul,' cried the enemy, rubbing his crimson ears. 'He savaged me on the ground.'

'You must take your chance of that,' said Lord Rufton coldly.

'Time,' cried Lord Sadler, and once again we advanced to the assault.

He was flushed, and his small eyes were as vicious as those of a bulldog. There was hatred on his face. For my part I carried myself lightly and gaily. A French gentleman fights, but he does not hate. I drew myself up before him, and I bowed as I have done in the duello. There can be grace and courtesy as well as defiance in a bow; I put all three into this one, with a touch of ridicule in the shrug which accompanied it. It was at this moment that he struck me. The room spun round with me. I fell upon my back. But in an instant I was on my feet again and had rushed to a close combat. His ear, his hair, his nose, I seized them each in turn. Once again the mad joy of the battle was in my veins. The old cry of triumph rose to my lips. 'Vive l'Empereur!' I yelled as I drove my head into his stomach. He threw his arm round my neck, and holding me with one hand he struck me with the other. I buried my teeth in his arm, and he shouted with pain. 'Call him off, Rufton!' he screamed. 'Call him off, man! He's worrying me!' They dragged me away from him. Can I ever forget it? – the laughter, the cheering, the congratulations! Even my enemy bore me no ill will, for he shook me by the hand. For my part I embraced him on each cheek. Five years afterwards I learned from Lord Rufton that my noble bearing upon that evening was still fresh in the memory of my English friends.

It is not, however, of my own exploits in sport that I wish to speak to you tonight, but it is of the Lady Jane Dacre and the strange adventure of which she was the cause. Lady Jane Dacre was Lord Rufton's sister and the lady of his household. I fear that until I came it was lonely for her, since she was a beautiful and refined woman with nothing in common with those who were about her. Indeed, this might be said of many women in the England of those days, for the men were rude and rough and coarse, with boorish habits and few accomplishments, while the women were the most lovely and tender that I have ever known. We became great friends, the Lady Jane and I, for it was not possible for me to drink three bottles of port after dinner like those Devonshire gentlemen, and so I would seek refuge in her drawing-room, where evening after evening she would play the harpsichord and I would sing the songs of my own land. In those peaceful moments I would find a refuge from the misery which filled me, when I reflected that my regiment was left in front of the enemy without the chief whom they had learned to love and to follow. Indeed, I could have torn my hair when I read in the English papers of the fine fighting which was going on in Portugal and on the frontiers of Spain, all of which I had missed through my misfortune in falling into the hands of Milord Wellington.

From what I have told you of the Lady Jane you will have guessed what occurred, my friends. Etienne Gerard is thrown into the company of a young and beautiful woman. What must it mean for him? What must it mean for her? It was not for me, the guest, the captive, to make love to the sister of my host. But I was reserved. I was discreet. I tried to curb my own emotions and to discourage hers. For my own part I fear that I betrayed myself, for the eye becomes more eloquent when the tongue is silent. Every quiver of my fingers as I turned over her music-sheets told her my secret. But she – she was admirable. It is in these matters that women have a genius for deception. If I had not penetrated her secret I should often have thought that she forgot even that I was in the house. For hours she would sit lost in a sweet melancholy, while I admired her pale face and her curls in the lamp-light, and thrilled within me to think that I had moved her so deeply. Then at last I would speak, and she would start in her chair and stare at me with the most admirable pretence of being surprised to find me in the room. Ah! how I longed to hurl myself suddenly at her feet, to kiss her white hand, to assure her that I had surprised her secret and that I would not abuse her confidence. But, no, I was not her equal, and I was under her roof as a castaway enemy. My lips were sealed. I endeavoured to imitate her own wonderful affectation of indifference, but, as you may think, I was eagerly alert for any opportunity of serving her.

One morning Lady Jane had driven in her phaeton to Okehampton, and I strolled along the road which led to that place in the hope that I might meet her on her return. It was the early winter, and banks of fading fern sloped down to the winding road. It is a bleak place this Dartmoor, wild and rocky – a country of wind and mist. I felt as I walked that it is no wonder Englishmen should suffer from the spleen. My own heart was heavy within me, and I sat upon a rock by the wayside looking out on the dreary view with my thoughts full of trouble and foreboding. Suddenly, however, as I glanced down the road I saw a sight which drove everything else from my mind, and caused me to leap to my feet with a cry of astonishment and anger.

Down the curve of the road a phaeton was coming, the pony tearing along at full gallop. Within was the very lady whom I had come to meet. She lashed at the pony like one who endeavours to escape from some pressing danger, glancing ever backwards over her shoulder. The bend of the road concealed from me what it was that had alarmed her, and I ran forward not knowing what to expect. The next instant I saw the pursuer, and my amazement was increased at the sight. It was a gentleman in the red coat of an English fox-hunter, mounted on a great grey horse. He was galloping as if in a race, and the long stride of the splendid creature beneath him soon brought him up to the lady's flying carriage. I saw him stoop and seize the reins of the pony, so as to bring it to a halt. The next instant he was deep in talk with the lady, he bending forward in his saddle and speaking eagerly, she shrinking away from him as if she feared and loathed him.

You may think, my dear friends, that this was not a sight at which I could calmly gaze. How my heart thrilled within me to think that a chance should have been given to me to serve the Lady Jane! I ran – oh, good Lord, how I ran! At last breathless, speechless, I reached the phaeton. The man glanced up at me with his blue English eyes, but so deep was he in his talk that he paid no heed to me, nor did the lady say a word. She still leaned back, her beautiful pale face gazing up at him. He was a good-looking fellow – tall, and strong, and brown; a pang of jealousy seized me as I looked at him. He was talking low and fast, as the English do when they are in earnest.

'I tell you, Jinny, it's you and only you that I love,' said he. 'Don't bear malice, Jinny. Let bygones be bygones. Come now, say it's all over.'

'No, never, George, never!' she cried.

A dusky red suffused his handsome face. The man was furious.

'Why can't you forgive me, Jinny?'

'I can't forget the past.'

'By George, you must! I've asked enough. It's time to order now. I'll have my rights. D'ye hear?' His hand closed upon her wrist.

At last my breath returned to me.

'Madame,' I said, as I raised my hat, 'do I intrude, or is there any possible way in which I can be of service to you?'

But neither of them minded me any more than if I had been a fly who buzzed between them. Their eyes were locked together.

'I'll have my rights, I tell you. I've waited long enough.'

'There's no use bullying, George.'

'Do you give in?'

'No, never!'

'Is that your final answer?'

'Yes, it is.'

He gave a bitter curse and threw down her hand.

'All right, my lady, we'll see about this.'

'Excuse me, sir,' said I, with dignity.

'Oh, go to blazes!' he cried, turning on me with his furious face. The next instant he had spurred his horse and was galloping down the road once more.

Lady Jane gazed after him until he was out of sight, and I was surprised to see that her face wore a smile and not a frown. Then she turned to me and held out her hand.

'You are very kind, Colonel Gerard. You meant well, I am sure.'

'Madame,' said I, 'if you can oblige me with the gentleman's name and address I will arrange that he shall never trouble you again.'

'No scandal, I beg of you,' she cried.

'Madame, I could not so far forget myself. Rest assured that no lady's name would ever be mentioned by me in the course of such an incident. In bidding me to go to blazes this gentleman has relieved me from the embarrassment of having to invent a cause of quarrel.'

'Colonel Gerard,' said the lady, earnestly, 'you must give me your word as a soldier and a gentleman that this matter goes no farther, and also that you will say nothing to my brother about what you have seen. Promise me!'

'If I must.'

'I hold you to your word. Now drive with me to High Combe, and I will explain as we go.'

The first words of her explanation went into me like a sabre-point.

'That gentleman,' said she, 'is my husband.'

'Your husband!'

'You must have known that I was married.' She seemed surprised at my agitation.

'I did not know.'

'He is Lord George Dacre. We have been married two years. There is no need to tell you how he wronged me. I left him and sought a refuge under my brother's roof. Up till today he has left me there unmolested. What I must above all things avoid is the chance of a duel betwixt my husband and my brother. It is horrible to think of. For this reason Lord Rufton must know nothing of this chance meeting of today.'

'If my pistol could free you from this annoyance—'

'No, no, it is not to be thought of. Remember your promise, Colonel Gerard. And not a word at High Combe of what you have seen!'

Her husband! I had pictured in my mind that she was a young widow. This brown-faced brute with his 'go to blazes' was the husband of this tender dove of a woman. Oh, if she would but allow me to free her from so odious an encumbrance! There is no divorce so quick and certain as that which I could give her. But a promise is a promise, and I kept it to the letter. My mouth was sealed. In a week I was to be sent back from Plymouth to St Malo, and it seemed to me that I might never hear the sequel of the story. And yet it was destined that it should have a sequel, and that I should play a very pleasing and honourable part in it.

*

It was only three days after the event which I have described when Lord Rufton burst hurriedly into my room. His face was pale, and his manner that of a man in extreme agitation.

'Gerard,' he cried, 'have you seen Lady Jane Dacre?'

I had seen her after breakfast, and it was now midday.

'By Heaven, there's villainy here!' cried my poor friend, rushing about like a madman. 'The bailiff has been up to say that a chaise and pair were seen driving full split down the Tavistock Road. The blacksmith heard a woman scream as it passed his forge. Jane has disappeared. By the Lord, I believe that she has been kidnapped by this villain Dacre.' He rang the bell furiously. 'Two horses this instant!' he cried. 'Colonel Gerard, your pistols! Jane comes back with me this night from Gravel Hanger, or there will be a new master in High Combe Hall.'

Behold us then within half an hour, like two knight-errants of old, riding forth to the rescue of this lady in distress. It was near Tavistock that Lord Dacre lived, and at every house and toll-gate along the road we heard the news of the flying post-chaise in front of us, so there could be no doubt whither they were bound. As we rode Lord Rufton told me of the man whom we were pursuing. His name, it seems, was a household word throughout all England for every sort of mischief. Wine, women, dice, cards, racing – in all forms of debauchery he had earned for himself a terrible name. He was of an old and noble family, and it had been hoped that he had sowed his wild oats when he married the beautiful Lady Jane Rufton. For some months he had indeed behaved well, and then he had wounded her feelings in their most tender part by some unworthy *liaison*. She had fled from his house and taken refuge with her brother, from whose care she had now been dragged once more, against her will. I ask you if two men could have had a fairer errand than that upon which Lord Rufton and myself were riding?

'That's Gravel Hanger,' he cried at last, pointing with his crop; and there on the green side of a hill was an old brick and timber building as beautiful as only an English country house can be. 'There's an inn by the park-gate, and there we shall leave our horses,' he added.

For my own part it seemed to me that with so just a cause we should have done best to ride boldly up to his door and summon him to surrender the lady. But there I was wrong. For the one thing which every Englishman fears is the law. He makes it himself, and when he has once made it it becomes a terrible tyrant before whom the bravest quails. He will smile at breaking his neck, but he will turn pale at breaking the law. It seems, then, from what Lord Rufton told me as we walked through the park, that we were on the wrong side of the law in this matter. Lord Dacre was in the right in carrying off his wife, since she did indeed belong to him, and our own position now was nothing better than that of burglars and trespassers. It was not for burglars to openly approach the front door. We could take the lady by force or by craft, but we could not take her by right, for the law was against us. This was what my friend explained to me as we crept up towards the shelter of a shrubbery which was close to the windows of the house. Thence we could examine this fortress, see whether we could effect a lodgment in it, and, above all, try to establish some communication with the beautiful prisoner inside.

There we were, then, in the shrubbery, Lord Rufton and I, each with a pistol in the pockets of our riding-coats, and with the most resolute determination in our hearts that we should not return without the lady. Eagerly we scanned every window of the wide-spread house. Not a sign could we see of the prisoner or of anyone else; but on the gravel drive outside the door were the deep-sunk marks of the wheels of the chaise. There was no doubt that they had arrived. Crouching among the laurel bushes we held a whispered council of war, but a singular interruption brought it to an end.

Out of the door of the house there stepped a tall, flaxen-haired man, such a figure as one would choose for the flank of a Grenadier company. As he turned his brown face and his blue eyes towards us I recognized Lord Dacre. With long strides he came down the gravel path straight for the spot where we lay.

'Come out, Ned!' he shouted; 'you'll have the game-keeper putting a charge of shot into you. Come out, man, and don't skulk behind the bushes.'

It was not a very heroic situation for us. My poor friend

rose with a crimson face. I sprang to my feet also and bowed with such dignity as I could muster.

'Halloa! it's the Frenchman is it?' said he, without returning my bow. 'I've got a crow to pluck with him already. As to you, Ned, I knew you would be hot on our scent, and so I was looking out for you. I saw you cross the park and go to ground in the shrubbery. Come in, man, and let us have all the cards on the table.'

He seemed master of the situation, this handsome giant of a man, standing at his ease on his own ground while we slunk out of our hiding-place. Lord Rufton had said not a word, but I saw by his darkened brow and his sombre eyes that the storm was gathering. Lord Dacre led the way into the house, and we followed close at his heels. He ushered us himself into an oak-panelled sitting-room, closing the door behind us. Then he looked me up and down with insolent eyes.

'Look here, Ned,' said he, 'time was when an English family could settle their own affairs in their own way. What has this foreign fellow got to do with your sister and my wife?'

'Sir,' said I, 'permit me to point out to you that this is not a case merely of a sister or a wife, but that I am a friend of the lady in question, and that I have the privilege which every gentleman possesses of protecting a woman against brutality. It is only by a gesture that I can show you what I think of you.' I had my riding-glove in my hand, and I flicked him across the face with it. He drew back with a bitter smile and his eyes were as hard as flint.

'So you've brought your bully with you, Ned?' said he. 'You might at least have done your fighting yourself, if it must come to a fight.'

'So I will,' cried Lord Rufton. 'Here and now.'

'When I've killed this swaggering Frenchman,' said Lord Dacre. He stepped to a side table and opened a brass-bound case. 'By Gad,' said he, 'either that man or I go out of this room feet foremost. I meant well by you, Ned; I did, by

George, but I'll shoot this led-captain of yours as sure as my name's George Dacre. Take your choice of pistols, sir, and shoot across this table. The barkers are loaded. Aim straight and kill me if you can, for, by the Lord, if you don't, you're done.'

In vain Lord Rufton tried to take the quarrel upon himself. Two things were clear in my mind – one that the Lady Jane had feared above all things that her husband and brother should fight, the other that if I could but kill this big milord, then the whole question would be settled for ever in the best way. Lord Rufton did not want him. Lady Jane did not want him. Therefore, I, Etienne Gerard, their friend, would pay the debt of gratitude which I owed them by freeing them of this encumbrance. But, indeed, there was no choice in the matter, for Lord Dacre was as eager to put a bullet into me as I could be to do the same service to him. In vain Lord Rufton argued and scolded. The affair must continue.

'Well, if you must fight my guest instead of myself, let it be tomorrow morning with two witnesses,' he cried at last; 'this is sheer murder across the table.'

'But it suits my humour, Ned,' said Lord Dacre.

'And mine, sir,' said I.

'Then I'll have nothing to do with it,' cried Lord Rufton. 'I tell you, George, if you shoot Colonel Gerard under these circumstances you'll find yourself in the dock instead of on the bench. I won't act as second, and that's flat.'

'Sir,' said I, 'I am perfectly prepared to proceed without a second.'

'That won't do. It's against the law,' cried Lord Dacre. 'Come, Ned, don't be a fool. You see we mean to fight. Hang it, man, all I want you to do is to drop a handkerchief.'

'I'll take no part in it.'

'Then I must find someone who will,' said Lord Dacre. He threw a cloth over the pistols, which lay upon the table, and he rang the bell. A footman entered. 'Ask Colonel Berkeley if he will step this way. You will find him in the billiard-room.'

A moment later there entered a tall thin Englishman with a great moustache, which was a rare thing amid that clean-shaven race. I have heard since that they were worn only by the Guards and the Hussars. This Colonel Berkeley was a guardsman. He seemed a strange, tired, languid, drawling creature with a long black cigar thrusting out, like a pole from a bush, amidst that immense moustache. He looked from one to the other of us with true English phlegm, and he betrayed not the slightest surprise when he was told our intention.

'Quite so,' said he; 'quite so.'

'I refuse to act, Colonel Berkeley,' cried Lord Rufton. 'Remember, this duel cannot proceed without you, and I hold you personally responsible for anything that happens.'

This Colonel Berkeley appeared to be an authority upon the question, for he removed the cigar from his mouth and he laid down the law in his strange, drawling voice.

'The circumstances are unusual, but not irregular, Lord Rufton,' said he. 'This gentleman has given a blow, and this other gentleman has received it. That is a clear issue. Time and conditions depend upon the person who demands satisfaction. Very good. He claims it here and now, across the table. He is acting within his rights. I am prepared to accept the responsibility.'

There was nothing more to be said. Lord Rufton sat moodily in the corner, with his brows drawn down and his hands thrust deep into the pockets of his riding-breeches. Colonel Berkeley examined the two pistols and laid them both in the centre of the table. Lord Dacre was at one end and I at the other, with eight feet of shining mahogany between us. On the hearthrug, with his back to the fire, stood the tall colonel, his handkerchief in his left hand, his cigar between two fingers of his right.

'When I drop the handkerchief,' said he, 'you will pick up your pistols and you will fire at your own convenience. Are you ready?'

'Yes,' we cried.

His hand opened, and the handkerchief fell. I bent swiftly

forward and seized a pistol, but the table, as I have said, was eight feet across, and it was easier for this long-armed milord to reach the pistols than it was for me. I had not yet drawn myself straight before he fired, and to this it was that I owe my life. His bullet would have blown out my brains had I been erect. As it was it whistled through my curls. At the same instant, just as I threw up my own pistol to fire, the door flew open, and a pair of arms were thrown round me. It was the beautiful, flushed, frantic face of Lady Jane which looked up into mine.

'You shan't fire! Colonel Gerard, for my sake, don't fire,' she cried. 'It is a mistake, I tell you – a mistake, a mistake! He is the best and dearest of husbands. Never again shall I leave his side.' Her hands slid down my arm and closed upon my pistol.

'Jane, Jane,' cried Lord Rufton; 'come with me. You should not be here. Come away.'

'It is all confoundedly irregular,' said Colonel Berkeley.

'Colonel Gerard, you won't fire, will you? My heart would break if he were hurt.'

'Hang it all, Jinny, give the fellow fair play,' cried Lord Dacre. 'He stood my fire like a man, and I won't see him interfered with. Whatever happens, I can't get worse than I deserve.'

But already there had passed between me and the lady a quick glance of the eyes which told her everything. Her hands slipped from my arm. 'I leave my husband's life and my own happiness to Colonel Gerard,' said she.

How well she knew me, this admirable woman! I stood for an instant irresolute, with the pistol cocked in my hand. My antagonist faced me bravely, with no blenching of his sunburnt face and no flinching of his bold, blue eyes.

'Come, come, sir, take your shot!' cried the colonel from the mat.

'Let us have it, then,' said Lord Dacre.

I would, at least, show them how completely his life was at the mercy of my skill. So much I owed to my own self-respect. I glanced round for a mark. The colonel was looking towards my antagonist, expecting to see him drop. His face was sideways to me, his long cigar projecting from his lips with an inch of ash at the end of it. Quick as a flash I raised my pistol and fired.

'Permit me to trim your ash, sir,' said I, and I bowed with a grace which is unknown among these islanders.

I am convinced that the fault lay with the pistol and not with my aim. I could hardly believe my own eyes when I saw that I had snapped off the cigar within half an inch of his lips. He stood staring at me with the ragged stub of the cigar-end sticking out from his singed moustache. I can see him now with his foolish, angry eyes and his long, thin, puzzled face. Then he began to talk. I have always said that the English are not really a phlegmatic or a taciturn nation if you stir them out of their groove. No one could have talked in a more animated way than this colonel. Lady Jane put her hands over her ears.

'Come, come, Colonel Berkeley,' said Lord Dacre, sternly, 'you forget yourself. There is a lady in the room.'

The colonel gave a stiff bow.

'If Lady Dacre will kindly leave this room,' said he, 'I will be able to tell this infernal little Frenchman what I think of him and his monkey tricks.'

I was splendid at that moment, for I ignored the words that he had said and remembered only the extreme provocation.

'Sir,' said I, 'I freely offer you my apologies for this unhappy incident. I felt that if I did not discharge my pistol Lord Dacre's honour might feel hurt, and yet it was quite impossible for me, after hearing what this lady had said, to aim it at her husband. I looked round for a mark, therefore, and I had the extreme misfortune to blow your cigar out of your mouth when my intention had merely been to snuff the ash. I was betrayed by my pistol. This is my explanation, sir, and if after listening to my apologies you still feel that I owe you satisfaction, I need not say that it is a request which I am unable to refuse.'

It was certainly a charming attitude which I had assumed,

and it won the hearts of all of them. Lord Dacre stepped forward and wrung me by the hand. 'By George, sir,' said he, 'I never thought to feel towards a Frenchman as I do to you. You're a man and a gentleman, and I can't say more.' Lord Rufton said nothing, but his handgrip told me all that he thought. Even Colonel Berkeley paid me a compliment, and declared that he would think no more about the unfortunate cigar. And she – ah, if you could have seen the look she gave me, the flushed cheek, the moist eye, the tremulous lip! When I think of my beautiful Lady Jane it is at that moment that I recall her. They would have had me stay to dinner, but you will understand, my friends, that this was no time for either Lord Rufton or myself to remain at Gravel Hanger. This reconciled couple desired only to be alone. In the chaise he had persuaded her of his sincere repentance, and once again they were a loving husband and wife. If they were to remain so, it was best perhaps that I should go. Why should I unsettle that domestic peace? Even against my own will my mere presence and appearance might have their effect upon the lady. No, no, I must tear myself away – even her persuasions were unable to make me stop. Years afterwards I heard that the household of the Dacres was among the happiest in the country, and that no cloud had ever come again to darken their lives. Yet I dare say if he could have seen into his wife's mind – but there, I say no more! A lady's secret is her own, and I fear that she and it are buried long years ago in some Devonshire churchyard. Perhaps all that gay circle are gone and the Lady Jane only lives now in the memory of an old half-pay French brigadier. He at least can never forget.

6 How the Brigadier rode to Minsk

I would have a stronger wine tonight, my friends, a wine of Burgundy rather than of Bordeaux. It is that my heart, my old soldier heart, is heavy within me. It is a strange thing, this age which creeps upon one. One does not know, one does not understand; the spirit is ever the same, and one does not remember how the poor body crumbles. But there comes a moment when it is brought home, when quick as the sparkle of a whirling sabre it is clear to us, and we see the men we were and the men we are. Yes, yes, it was so today, and I would have a wine of Burgundy tonight, White Burgundy – Montrachet — Sir, I am your debtor!

It was this morning in the Champ de Mars. Your pardon, friends, while an old man tells his trouble. You saw the review. Was it not splendid? I was in the enclosure for veteran officers who have been decorated. This ribbon on my breast was my passport. The cross itself I keep at home in a leathern pouch. They did us honour, for we were placed at the saluting point, with the Emperor and the carriages of the Court upon our right.

It is years since I have been to a review, for I cannot approve of many things which I have seen. I do not approve of the red breeches of the infantry. It was in white breeches that the infantry used to fight. Red is for the cavalry. A little more, and they would ask our busbies and our spurs! Had I been seen at a review they might well have said that I, Etienne Gerard, had condoned it. So I have stayed at home. But this war of the Crimea is different. The men go to battle. It is not for me to be absent when brave men gather.

My faith, they march well, those little infantrymen! They are not large, but they are very solid and they carry themselves well. I took off my hat to them as they passed. Then there came the guns. They were good guns, well horsed, and well manned. I took off my hat to them. Then came the

Engineers, and to them also I took off my hat. There are no braver men than the Engineers. Then came the cavalry, Lancers, Cuirassiers, Chasseurs, and Spahis. To all of them in turn I was able to take off my hat, save only to the Spahis. The Emperor had no Spahis. But when all of the others had passed, what think you came at the close? A brigade of Hussars, and at the charge! Oh, my friends, the pride and the glory and the beauty, the flash and the sparkle, the roar of the hoofs, and the jingle of chains, the tossing manes, the noble heads, the rolling cloud, and the dancing waves of steel! My heart drummed to them as they passed. And the last of all, was it not my own old regiment? My eyes fell upon the grey and silver dolmans, with the leopard-skin schabraques, and at that instant the years fell away from me and I saw my own beautiful men and horses, even as they had swept behind their young colonel, in the pride of our youth and strength, just forty years ago. Up flew my cane. '*Chargez! En avant! Vive l'Empereur!*' It was the past calling to the present. But, oh, what a thin, piping voice! Was this the voice that had once thundered from wing to wing of a strong brigade? And the arm that could scarce wave a cane, were these the muscles of fire and steel which had no match in all Napoleon's mighty host? They smiled at me. They cheered me. The Emperor laughed and bowed. But to me the present was a dim dream, and what was real were my eight hundred dead Hussars and the Etienne of long ago. Enough – a brave man can face age and fate as he faced Cossacks and Uhlans. But there are times when Montrachet is better than the wine of Bordeaux.

It is to Russia that they go, and so I will tell you a story of Russia. Ah, what an evil dream of the night it seems! Blood and ice. Ice and blood. Fierce faces with snow upon the whiskers. Blue hands held out for succour. And across the great white plain the one long black line of moving figures, trudging, trudging, a hundred miles, another hundred, and still always the same white plain. Sometimes there were fir-woods to limit it, sometimes it stretched away to the cold blue sky, but the black line stumbled on and on.

Those weary, ragged, starving men, the spirit frozen out of them, looked neither to right nor left, but with sunken faces and rounded backs trailed onwards and ever onwards, making for France as wounded beasts make for their lair. There was no speaking, and you could scarce hear the shuffle of feet in the snow. Once only I heard them laugh. It was outside Wilna, when an aide-de-camp rode up to the head of that dreadful column and asked if that were the Grand Army. All who were within hearing looked round, and when they saw those broken men, those ruined regiments, those fur-capped skeletons who were once the Guard, they laughed, and the laugh crackled down the column like a *feu de joie*. I have heard many a groan and cry and scream in my life, but nothing so terrible as the laugh of the Grand Army.

But why was it that these helpless men were not destroyed by the Russians ? Why was it that they were not speared by the Cossacks or herded into droves, and driven as prisoners into the heart of Russia ? On every side as you watched the black snake winding over the snow you saw also the dark, moving shadows which came and went like cloud drifts on either flank and behind. They were the Cossacks, who hung round us like wolves round the flock. But the reason why they did not ride in upon us was that all the ice of Russia could not cool the hot hearts of some of our soldiers. To the end there were always those who were ready to throw themselves between these savages and their prey. One man above all rose greater as the danger thickened, and won a higher name amid disaster than he had done when he led our van to victory. To him I drink this glass – to Ney, the red-maned Lion, glaring back over his shoulder at the enemy who feared to tread too closely on his heels. I can see him now, his broad white face convulsed with fury, his light blue eyes sparkling like flints, his great voice roaring and crashing amid the roll of the musketry. His glazed and featherless cocked hat was the ensign upon which France rallied during those dreadful days.

It is well known that neither I nor the regiment of

Hussars of Conflans were at Moscow. We were left behind on the lines of communication at Borodino. How the Emperor could have advanced without us is incomprehensible to me, and, indeed, it was only then that I understood that his judgement was weakening, and that he was no longer the man that he had been. However, a soldier has to obey orders, and so I remained at this village, which was poisoned by the bodies of thirty thousand men who had lost their lives in the great battle. I spent the late autumn in getting my horses into condition and reclothing my men, so that when the army fell back on Borodino my Hussars were the best of the cavalry, and were placed under Ney in the rear-guard. What could he have done without us during those dreadful days? 'Ah, Gerard,' said he one evening – but it is not for me to repeat the words. Suffice it that he spoke what the whole army felt. The rear-guard covered the army, and the Hussars of Conflans covered the rear-guard. There was the whole truth in a sentence. Always the Cossacks were on us. Always we held them off. Never a day passed that we had not to wipe our sabres. That was soldiering indeed.

But there came a time between Wilna and Smolensk when the situation became impossible. Cossacks and even cold we could fight, but we could not fight hunger as well. Food must be got at all costs. That night Ney sent for me to the waggon in which he slept. His great head was sunk on his hands. Mind and body, he was wearied to death.

'Colonel Gerard,' said he, 'things are going very badly with us. The men are starving. We must have food at all costs.'

'The horses,' I suggested.

'Save your handful of cavalry, there are none left.'

'The band,' said I.

He laughed, even in his despair.

'Why the band?' he asked.

'Fighting men are of value.'

'Good!' said he. 'You would play the game down to the

last card, and so would I. Good, Gerard, good!' He clasped my hand in his. 'But there is one chance for us yet, Gerard.' He unhooked a lantern from the roof of the waggon, and he laid it on a map which was stretched before him. 'To the south of us,' said he, 'there lies the town of Minsk. I have word from a Russian deserter that much corn has been stored in the town-hall. I wish you to take as many men as you think best, set forth for Minsk, seize the corn, load any carts which you may collect in the town, and bring them to me between here and Smolensk. If you fail, it is but a detachment cut off. If you succeed, it is new life to the army.'

He had not expressed himself well, for it was evident that if we failed it was not merely the loss of a detachment. It is quality as well as quantity which counts. And yet how honourable a mission, and how glorious a risk! If mortal men could bring it, then the corn should come from Minsk. I said so, and spoke a few burning words about a brave man's duty until the Marshal was so moved that he rose and, taking me affectionately by the shoulders, pushed me out of the waggon.

It was clear to me that in order to succeed in my enterprise I should take a small force and depend rather upon surprise than upon numbers. A large body could not conceal itself, would have great difficulty in getting food, and would cause all the Russians around us to concentrate for its certain destruction. On the other hand, if a small body of cavalry could get past the Cossacks unseen it was probable that they would find no troops to oppose them, for we knew that the main Russian army was several days' march behind us. This corn was meant, no doubt, for their consumption. A squadron of Hussars and thirty Polish Lancers were all whom I chose for the venture. That very night we rode out of the camp, and struck south in the direction of Minsk.

Fortunately there was but half a moon, and we were able to pass without being attacked by the enemy. Twice we saw great fires burning amid the snow, and around them a thick bristle of long poles. These were the lances of Cossacks, which they had stood upright while they slept. It would have been a great joy to us to have charged in amongst them, for we had much to revenge, and the eyes of my comrades looked longingly from me to those red flickering patches in the darkness. My faith, I was sorely tempted to do it, for it would have been a good lesson to teach them that they must keep a few miles between themselves and a French army. It is the essence of good generalship, however, to keep one thing before one at a time, and so we rode silently on through the snow, leaving these Cossack bivouacs to right and left. Behind us the black sky was all mottled with a line of flame, which showed where our own poor wretches were trying to keep themselves alive for another day of misery and starvation.

All night we rode slowly onwards, keeping our horses' tails to the Pole Star. There were many tracks in the snow, and we kept to the line of these, that no one might remark that a body of cavalry had passed that way. These are the little precautions which mark the experienced officer. Besides, by keeping to the tracks we were most likely to find the villages, and only in the villages could we hope to get food. The dawn of day found us in a thick fir-wood, the trees so loaded with snow that the light could hardly reach us. When we had found our way out of it it was full daylight, the rim of the rising sun peeping over the edge of the great snow-plain and turning it crimson from end to end. I halted my Hussars and Lancers under the shadow of the wood, and I studied the country. Close to us there was a small farmhouse. Beyond, at a distance of several miles, was a village. Far away on the skyline rose a considerable town all bristling with church towers. This was Minsk. In no direction could I see any signs of troops. It was evident that we had passed through the Cossacks, and that there was nothing between us and our goal. A joyous shout burst from my men when I told them our position, and we advanced rapidly towards the village.

I have said, however, that there was a small farmhouse immediately in front of us. As we rode up to it I observed that a fine grey horse with a military saddle was tethered by the door. Instantly I galloped forward, but before I could reach it a man dashed out of the door, flung himself on to the horse, and rode furiously away, the crisp, dry snow flying up in a cloud behind him. The sunlight gleamed upon his gold epaulettes, and I knew that he was a Russian officer. He would raise the whole countryside if we did not catch him. I put spurs to Violette and flew after him. My troopers followed; but there was no horse among them to compare with Violette, and I knew well that if I could not catch the Russian I need expect no help from them.

But it is a swift horse indeed and a skilful rider who can hope to escape from Violette with Etienne Gerard in the saddle. He rode well, this young Russian, and his mount was a good one, but gradually we wore him down. His face glanced continually over his shoulder – a dark, handsome face, with eyes like an eagle – and I saw as I closed with him that he was measuring the distance between us. Suddenly he half turned; there were a flash and a crack as his pistol bullet hummed past my ear. Before he could draw his sword I was upon him; but he still spurred his horse, and the two galloped together over the plain, I with my leg against the Russian's and my left hand upon his right shoulder. I saw his hand fly up to his mouth. Instantly I dragged him across my pommel and seized him by the throat, so that he could not swallow. His horse shot from under him, but I held him fast, and Violette came to a stand. Sergeant Oudin of the Hussars was the first to join us. He was an old soldier, and he saw at a glance what I was after.

'Hold tight, Colonel,' said he; 'I'll do the rest.'

He slipped out his knife, thrust the blade between the clenched teeth of the Russian, and turned it so as to force his mouth open. There, on his tongue, was the little wad of wet paper which he had been so anxious to swallow. Oudin picked it out, and I let go of the man's throat. From the way in which, half strangled as he was, he glanced at the paper I was sure that it was a message of extreme importance. His hands twitched as if he longed to snatch it from me. He shrugged his shoulders, however, and smiled good-humouredly when I apologized for my roughness.

'And now to business,' said I, when he had done coughing and hawking. 'What is your name?'

'Alexis Barakoff.'

'Your rank and regiment?'

'Captain of the Dragoons of Grodno.'

'What is this note which you were carrying?'

'It is a line which I had written to my sweetheart.'

'Whose name,' said I, examining the address, 'is the Hetman Platoff. Come, come, sir, this is an important military document, which you are carrying from one general to another. Tell me this instant what it is.'

'Read it, and then you will know.' He spoke perfect French, as do most of the educated Russians. But he knew well that there is not one French officer in a thousand who knows a word of Russian. The inside of the note contained one single line which ran like this: –

Pustj Franzuzy pridutt v Minsk. Min gotovy.

I stared at it, and I had to shake my head. Then I showed it to my Hussars, but they could make nothing of it. The Poles were all rough fellows who could not read or write, save only the sergeant, who came from Memel, in East Prussia, and knew no Russian. It was maddening, for I felt that I had possession of some important secret upon which the safety of the army might depend, and yet I could make no sense of it. Again I entreated our prisoner to translate it, and offered him his freedom if he would do so. He only smiled at my request. I could not but admire him, for it was the very smile which I should have myself smiled had I been in his position.

'At least,' said I, 'tell us the name of this village.'

'It is Dobrova.'

'And that is Minsk over yonder I suppose?'

'Yes, that is Minsk.'

'Then we shall go to the village and we shall very soon find someone who will translate this despatch.'

So we rode onward together, a trooper with his carbine

on either side of our prisoner. The village was but a little place, and I set a guard at the ends of the single street, so that no one could escape from it. It was necessary to call a halt and to find some food for the men and horses, since they had travelled all night and had a long journey still before them.

There was one large stone house in the centre of the village, and to this I rode. It was the house of the priest – a snuffy and ill-favoured old man who had not a civil answer to any of our questions. An uglier fellow I never met, but, my faith, it was very different with his only daughter, who kept house for him. She was a brunette, a rare thing in Russia, with creamy skin, raven hair and a pair of the most glorious dark eyes that ever kindled at the sight of a Hussar. From the first glance I saw that she was mine. It was no time for love-making when a soldier's duty had to be done, but still, as I took the simple meal which they laid before me, I chatted lightly with the lady, and we were the best of friends before an hour had passed. Sophie was her first name, her second I never knew. I taught her to call me Etienne, and I tried to cheer her up, for her sweet face was sad and there were tears in her beautiful dark eyes. I pressed her to tell me what it was which was grieving her.

'How can I be otherwise,' said she, speaking French with a most adorable lisp, 'when one of my poor countrymen is a prisoner in your hands? I saw him between two of your Hussars as you rode into the village.'

'It is the fortune of war,' said I. 'His turn today; mine, perhaps, tomorrow.'

'But consider, Monsieur—' said she.

'Etienne,' said I.

'Well, then,' she cried, beautifully flushed and desperate, 'consider, Etienne, that this young officer will be taken back to your army and will be starved or frozen, for if, as I hear, your own soldiers have a hard march, what will be the lot of a prisoner?'

I shrugged my shoulders.

'You have a kind face, Etienne,' said she; 'you would not

condemn this poor man to certain death. I entreat you to let him go.'

Her delicate hand rested upon my sleeve, her dark eyes looked imploringly into mine.

A sudden thought passed through my mind. I would grant her request, but I would demand a favour in return. At my order the prisoner was brought up into the room.

'Captain Barakoff,' said I, 'this young lady has begged me to release you, and I am inclined to do so. I would ask you to give your parole that you will remain in this dwelling for twenty-four hours, and take no steps to inform anyone of our movements.'

'I will do so,' said he.

'Then I trust in your honour. One man more or less can make no difference in a struggle between great armies, and to take you back as a prisoner would be to condemn you to death. Depart, sir, and show your gratitude not to me, but to the first French officer who falls into your hands.'

When he was gone I drew my paper from my pocket.

'Now, Sophie,' said I, 'I have done what you asked me, and all that I ask in return is that you will give me a lesson in Russian.'

'With all my heart,' said she.

'Let us begin on this,' said I, spreading out the paper before her. 'Let us take it word for word and see what it means.'

She looked at the writing with some surprise. 'It means,' said she, 'if the French come to Minsk all is lost.' Suddenly a look of consternation passed over her beautiful face. 'Great heavens!' she cried, 'what is it that I have done? I have betrayed my country! Oh, Etienne, your eyes are the last for whom this message is meant. How could you be so cunning as to make a poor, simple-minded, and unsuspecting girl betray the cause of her country?'

I consoled my poor Sophie as best I might, and I assured her that it was no reproach to her that she should be outwitted by so old a campaigner and so shrewd a man as myself. But it was no time now for talk. This message made it clear that the corn was indeed at Minsk, and that there were no troops there to defend it. I gave a hurried order from the window, the trumpeter blew the assembly, and in ten minutes we had left the village behind us and were riding hard for the city, the gilded domes and minarets of which glimmered above the snow of the horizon. Higher they rose and higher, until at last, as the sun sank towards the west, we were in the broad main street, and galloped up it amid the shouts of the moujiks and the cries of frightened women until we found ourselves in front of the great town-hall. My cavalry I drew up in the square, and I, with my two sergeants, Oudin and Papilette, rushed into the building.

Heavens! shall I ever forget the sight which greeted us? Right in front of us was drawn up a triple line of Russian Grenadiers. Their muskets rose as we entered, and a crashing volley burst into our very faces. Oudin and Papilette dropped upon the floor, riddled with bullets. For myself, my busby was shot away and I had two holes through my dolman. The Grenadiers ran at me with their bayonets. 'Treason!' I cried. 'We are betrayed! Stand to your horses!' I rushed out of the hall, but the whole square was swarming with troops. From every side street Dragoons and Cossacks were riding down upon us, and such a rolling fire had burst from the surrounding houses that half my men and horses were on the ground. 'Follow me!' I yelled, and sprang upon Violette, but a giant of a Russian Dragoon officer threw his arms round me, and we rolled on the ground together. He shortened his sword to kill me, but, changing his mind, he seized me by the throat and banged my head against the stones until I was unconscious. So it was that I became the prisoner of the Russians.

When I came to myself my only regret was that my captor had not beaten out my brains. There in the grand square of Minsk lay half my troopers dead or wounded, with exultant crowds of Russians gathered round them. The rest, in a melancholy group, were herded into the porch of the town-hall, a *sotnia* of Cossacks keeping guard over them. Alas! what could I say, what could I do? It was evident that

I had led my men into a carefully baited trap. They had heard of our mission, and they had prepared for us. And yet there was that despatch which had caused me to neglect all precautions and to ride straight into the town. How was I to account for that? The tears ran down my cheeks as I surveyed the ruin of my squadron, and as I thought of the plight of my comrades of the Grand Army who awaited the food which I was to have brought them. Ney had trusted me, and I had failed him. How often he would strain his eyes over the snowfields for that convoy of grain which should never gladden his sight! My own fate was hard enough. An exile in Siberia was the best which the future could bring me. But you will believe me, my friends, that it was not for his own sake, but for that of his starving comrades, that Etienne Gerard's cheeks were lined by his tears, frozen even as they were shed.

'What's this?' said a gruff voice at my elbow; and I turned to face the huge, black-bearded Dragoon who had dragged me from my saddle. 'Look at the Frenchman crying! I thought that the Corsican was followed by brave men, and not by children.'

'If you and I were face to face and alone, I should let you see which is the better man,' said I.

For answer the brute struck me across the face with his open hand. I seized him by the throat, but a dozen of his soldiers tore me away from him, and he struck me again while they held my hands.

'You base hound,' I cried, 'is this the way to treat an officer and a gentleman?'

'We never asked you to come to Russia,' said he. 'If you do you must take such treatment as you can get. I would shoot you off-hand if I had my way.'

'You will answer for this some day,' I cried, as I wiped the blood from my moustache.

'If the Hetman Platoff is of my way of thinking you will not be alive this time tomorrow,' he answered, with a ferocious scowl. He added some words in Russian to his troops, and instantly they all sprang to their saddles. Poor

Violette, looking as miserable as her master, was led round and I was told to mount her. My left arm was tied with a thong which was fastened to the stirrup-iron of a sergeant of Dragoons. So in most sorry plight I and the remnant of my men set forth from Minsk.

Never have I met such a brute as this man Sergine, who commanded the escort. The Russian army contains the best and the worst in the world, but a worse than Major Sergine of the Dragoons of Kieff I have never seen in any force outside of the guerillas of the Peninsula. He was a man of great stature, with a fierce, hard face and a bristling black beard, which fell over his cuirass. I have been told since that he was noted for his strength and his bravery, and I could answer for it that he had the grip of a bear, for I had felt it when he tore me from my saddle. He was a wit, too, in his way, and made continual remarks in Russian at our expense which set all his Dragoons and Cossacks laughing. Twice he beat my comrades with his riding-whip, and once he approached me with the lash swung over his shoulder, but there was something in my eyes which prevented it from falling. So in misery and humiliation, cold and starving, we rode in a disconsolate column across the vast snow-plain. The sun had sunk, but still in the long northern twilight we pursued our weary journey. Numbed and frozen, with my head aching from the blows it had received, I was borne onwards by Violette, hardly conscious of where I was or whither I was going. The little mare walked with a sunken head, only raising it to snort her contempt for the mangy Cossack ponies who were round her.

But suddenly the escort stopped, and I found that we had halted in the single street of a small Russian village. There was a church on one side, and on the other was a large stone house, the outline of which seemed to me to be familiar. I looked around me in the twilight, and then I saw that we had been led back to Dobrova, and that this house at the door of which we were waiting was the same house of the priest at which we had stopped in the morning. Here it was that my charming Sophie in her innocence had translated the unlucky message which had in some strange way led us to our ruin. To think that only a few hours before we had left this very spot with such high hopes and all fair prospects for our mission, and now the remnants of us waited as beaten and humiliated men for whatever lot a brutal enemy might ordain! But such is the fate of the soldier, my friends – kisses today, blows tomorrow. Tokay in a palace, ditch-water in a hovel, furs or rags, a full purse or an empty pocket, ever swaying from the best to the worst, with only his courage and his honour unchanging.

The Russian horsemen dismounted, and my poor fellows were ordered to do the same. It was already late, and it was clearly their intention to spend the night in this village. There were great cheering and joy amongst the peasants when they understood that we had all been taken, and they flocked out of their houses with flaming torches, the women carrying out tea and brandy for the Cossacks. Amongst others, the old priest came forth – the same whom we had seen in the morning. He was all smiles now, and he bore with him some hot punch on a salver, the reek of which I can remember still. Behind her father was Sophie. With horror I saw her clasp Major Sergine's hand as she congratulated him upon the victory he had won and the prisoners he had made. The old priest, her father, looked at me with an insolent face, and made insulting remarks at my expense, pointing at me with his lean and grimy hand. His fair daughter Sophie looked at me also, but she said nothing, and I could read her tender pity in her dark eyes. At last she turned to Major Sergine and said something to him in Russian, on which he frowned and shook his head impatiently. She appeared to plead with him, standing there in the flood of light which shone from the open door of her father's house. My eyes were fixed upon the two faces, that of the beautiful girl and of the dark, fierce man, for my instinct told me that it was my own fate which was under debate. For a long time the soldier shook his head, and then, at last softening before her pleadings, he appeared to give way. He turned to where I stood with my guardian sergeant beside me.

'These good people offer you the shelter of their roof for the night,' said he to me, looking me up and down with vindictive eyes. 'I find it hard to refuse them, but I tell you straight that for my part I had rather see you on the snow. It would cool your hot blood, you rascal of a Frenchman!'

I looked at him with the contempt that I felt.

'You were born a savage, and you will die one,' said I.

My words stung him, for he broke into an oath, raising his whip as if he would strike me.

'Silence, you crop-eared dog!' he cried. 'Had I my way some of the insolence would be frozen out of you before morning.' Mastering his passion, he turned upon Sophie with what he meant to be a gallant manner. 'If you have a cellar with a good lock,' said he, 'the fellow may lie in it for the night, since you have done him the honour to take an interest in his comfort. I must have his parole that he will not attempt to play us any tricks, as I am answerable for him until I hand him over to the Hetman Platoff tomorrow.'

His supercilious manner was more than I could endure. He had evidently spoken French to the lady in order that I might understand the humiliating way in which he referred to me.

'I will take no favour from you,' said I. 'You may do what you like, but I will never give you my parole.'

The Russian shrugged his great shoulders, and turned away as if the matter were ended.

'Very well, my fine fellow, so much the worse for your fingers and toes. We shall see how you are in the morning after a night in the snow.'

'One moment, Major Sergine,' cried Sophie. 'You must not be so hard upon this prisoner. There are some special reasons why he has a claim upon our kindness and mercy.'

The Russian looked with suspicion upon his face from her to me.

'What are the special reasons? You certainly seem to take

a remarkable interest in this Frenchman,' said he.

'The chief reason is that he has this very morning of his own accord released Captain Alexis Barakoff, of the Dragoons of Grodno.'

'It is true,' said Barakoff, who had come out of the house. 'He captured me this morning, and he released me upon parole rather than take me back to the French army, where I should have been starved.'

'Since Colonel Gerard has acted so generously you will surely, now that fortune has changed, allow us to offer him the poor shelter of our cellar upon this bitter night,' said Sophie. 'It is a small return for his generosity.'

But the Dragoon was still in the sulks.

'Let him give me his parole first that he will not attempt to escape,' said he. 'Do you hear, sir? Do you give me your parole?'

'I give you nothing,' said I.

'Colonel Gerard,' cried Sophie, turning to me with a coaxing smile, 'you will give *me* your parole, will you not?'

'To you, mademoiselle, I can refuse nothing. I will give you my parole, with pleasure.'

'There, Major Sergine,' cried Sophie, in triumph, 'that is surely sufficient. You have heard him say that he gives me his parole. I will be answerable for his safety.'

In an ungracious fashion my Russian bear grunted his consent, and so I was led into the house, followed by the scowling father and by the big, black-bearded Dragoon. In the basement there was a large and roomy chamber, where the winter logs were stored. Thither it was that I was led, and I was given to understand that this was to be my lodging for the night. One side of this bleak apartment was heaped up to the ceiling with faggots of firewood. The rest of the room was stone-flagged and bare-walled, with a single, deep-set window upon one side, which was safely guarded with iron bars. For light I had a large stable lantern, which swung from a beam of the low ceiling. Major Sergine smiled as he took this down, and swung it round so as to throw its light into every corner of that dreary chamber.

'How do you like our Russian hotels, monsieur?' he asked, with his hateful sneer. 'They are not very grand, but they are the best that we can give you. Perhaps the next time that you Frenchmen take a fancy to travel you will choose some other country where they will make you more comfortable.' He stood laughing at me, his white teeth gleaming through his beard. Then he left me, and I heard the great key creak in the lock.

For an hour of utter misery, chilled in body and soul, I sat upon a pile of faggots, my face sunk upon my hands and my mind full of the saddest thoughts. It was cold enough within those four walls, but I thought of the sufferings of my poor troopers outside, and I sorrowed with their sorrow. Then I paced up and down, and I clapped my hands together and kicked my feet against the walls to keep them from being frozen. The lamp gave out some warmth, but still it was bitterly cold, and I had had no food since morning. It seemed to me that everyone had forgotten me, but at last I heard the key turn in the lock, and who should enter but my prisoner of the morning, Captain Alexis Barakoff. A bottle of wine projected from under his arm, and he carried a great plate of hot stew in front of him.

'Hush!' said he; 'not a word! Keep up your heart! I cannot stop to explain, for Sergine is still with us. Keep awake and ready!' With these hurried words he laid down the welcome food and ran out of the room.

'Keep awake and ready!' The words rang in my ears. I ate my food and I drank my wine, but it was neither food nor wine which had warmed the heart within me. What could those words of Barakoff mean? Why was I to remain awake? For what was I to be ready? Was it possible that there was a chance yet of escape? I have never respected the man who neglects his prayers at all other times and yet prays when he is in peril. It is like a bad soldier who pays no respect to the colonel save when he would demand a favour of him. And yet when I thought of the salt-mines of Siberia on the one side and of my mother in France upon the other, I could not help a prayer rising not from my lips, but from my heart, that the words of Barakoff might mean all that I hoped. But hour after hour struck upon the village clock, and still I heard nothing save the call of the Russian sentries in the street outside.

Then at last my heart leaped within me, for I heard a light step in the passage. An instant later the key turned, the door opened, and Sophie was in the room.

'Monsieur—' she cried.

'Etienne,' said I.

'Nothing will change you,' said she. 'But is it possible that you do not hate me? Have you forgiven me the trick which I played you?'

'What trick?' I asked.

'Good heavens! is it possible that even now you have not understood it? You asked me to translate the despatch. I have told you that it meant, "If the French come to Minsk all is lost."'

'What did it mean, then?'

'It means, "Let the French come to Minsk. We are awaiting them."'

I sprang back from her.

'You betrayed me!' I cried. 'You lured me into this trap. It is to you that I owe the death and capture of my men. Fool that I was to trust a woman!'

'Do not be unjust, Colonel Gerard. I am a Russian woman, and my first duty is to my country. Would you not wish a French girl to have acted as I have done? Had I translated the message correctly you would not have gone to Minsk and your squadron would have escaped. Tell me that you forgive me!'

She looked bewitching as she stood pleading her cause in front of me. And yet, as I thought of my dead men, I could not take the hand which she held out to me.

'Very good,' said she, as she dropped it by her side. 'You feel for your own people and I feel for mine, and so we are equal. But you have said one wise and kindly thing within these walls, Colonel Gerard. You have said, "One man more or less can make no difference in a struggle between two great armies." Your lesson of nobility is not wasted. Behind those faggots is an unguarded door. Here is the key to it. Go forth, Colonel Gerard, and I trust that we may never look upon each other's faces again.'

I stood for an instant with the key in my hand and my head in a whirl. Then I handed it back to her.

'I cannot do it,' I said.

'Why not?'

'I have given my parole.'

'To whom?' she asked.

'Why, to you.'

'And I release you from it.'

My heart bounded with joy. Of course, it was true what she said. I had refused to give my parole to Sergine. I owed him no duty. If she relieved me from my promise my honour was clear. I took the key from her hand.

'You will find Captain Barakoff at the end of the village street,' she said. 'We of the North never forget either an injury or a kindness. He has your mare and your sword waiting for you. Do not delay an instant, for in two hours it will be dawn.'

So I passed out into the starlit Russian night, and had that last glimpse of Sophie as she peered after me through the open door. She looked wistfully at me as if she expected something more than the cold thanks which I gave her, but even the humblest man has his pride, and I will not deny that mine was hurt by the deception which she had played upon me. I could not have brought myself to kiss her hand, far less her lips. The door led into a narrow alley, and at the end of it stood a muffled figure who held Violette by the bridle.

'You told me to be kind to the next French officer whom I found in distress,' said he. 'Good luck! Bon voyage!' he whispered, as I bounded into the saddle. 'Remember "Poltava" is the watchword.'

It was well that he had given it to me, for twice I had to pass Cossack pickets before I was clear of the lines. I had just ridden past the last vedettes and hoped that I was a free man again when there was a soft thudding in the snow behind me, and a heavy man upon a great black horse came swiftly after me. My first impulse was to put spurs to Violette. My second, as I saw a long black beard against a steel cuirass, was to halt and await him.

'I thought that it was you, you dog of a Frenchman,' he cried, shaking his drawn sword at me. 'So you have broken your parole, you rascal?'

'I gave no parole.'

'You lie, you hound!'

I looked around and no one was coming. The vedettes were motionless and distant. We were all alone, with the moon above and the snow beneath. Fortune has ever been my friend.

'I gave you no parole.'

'You gave it to the lady.'

'Then I will answer for it to the lady.'

'That would suit you better, no doubt. But, unfortunately, you will have to answer for it to me.'

'I am ready.'

'Your sword, too! There is treason in this! Ah, I see it all! The woman has helped you. She shall see Siberia for this night's work.'

The words were his death-warrant. For Sophie's sake I could not let him go back alive. Our blades crossed, and an instant later mine was through his black beard and deep in his throat. I was on the ground almost as soon as he, but the one thrust was enough. He died, snapping his teeth at my ankles like a savage wolf.

Two days later I had rejoined the army at Smolensk, and was a part once more of that dreary procession which tramped onwards through the snow, leaving a long weal of blood to show the path which it had taken.

Enough, my friends; I would not reawaken the memory of those days of misery and death. They still come to haunt me in my dreams. When we halted at last in Warsaw, we had left behind us our guns, our transport, three-fourths of our comrades. But we did not leave behind us the honour of

Etienne Gerard. They have said that I broke my parole. Let them beware how they say it to my face, for the story is as I tell it, and old as I am my forefinger is not too weak to press a trigger when my honour is in question.

7 How the Brigadier bore himself at Waterloo

1 The story of the forest inn

Of all the great battles in which I had the honour of drawing my sword for the Emperor and for France there was not one which was lost. At Waterloo, although, in a sense, I was present, I was unable to fight, and the enemy was victorious. It is not for me to say that there is a connection between these two things. You know me too well, my friends, to imagine that I would make such a claim. But it gives matter for thought, and some have drawn flattering conclusions from it. After all, it was only a matter of breaking a few English squares and the day would have been our own. If the Hussars of Conflans, with Etienne Gerard to lead them, could not do this, then the best judges are mistaken. But let that pass. The Fates had ordained that I should hold my hand and that the Empire should fall. But they had also ordained that this day of gloom and sorrow should bring such honour to me as had never come when I swept on the wings of victory from Boulogne to Vienna. Never had I burned so brilliantly as at that supreme moment when the darkness fell upon all around me. You are aware that I was faithful to the Emperor in his adversity, and that I refused to sell my sword and my honour to the Bourbons. Never again was I to feel my war horse between my knees, never again to hear the kettledrums and silver trumpets behind me as I rode in front of my little rascals. But it comforts my heart, my friends, and it brings the tears to my eyes, to think how great I was upon that last day of my soldier life, and to remember that of all the remarkable exploits which have won me the love of so many beautiful women, and the respect of so many noble men, there was none which, in splendour, in audacity, and in the great end which was attained, could compare with my famous ride upon the night of June 18th, 1815. I am aware that the story is often told at mess-tables and in barrack-rooms, so that there are few in the army who have not heard it, but modesty has sealed my lips, until now, my friends, in the privacy of these intimate gatherings, I am inclined to lay the true facts before you.

In the first place, there is one thing which I can assure you. In all his career Napoleon never had so splendid an army as that with which he took the field for that campaign. In 1813 France was exhausted. For every veteran there were five children – Marie Louises as we called them, for the Empress had busied herself in raising levies while the Emperor took the field. But it was very different in 1815. The prisoners had all come back – the men from the snows of Russia, the men from the dungeons of Spain, the men from the hulks in England. These were the dangerous men, veterans of twenty battles, longing for their old trade, and with hearts filled with hatred and revenge. The ranks were full of soldiers who wore two and three chevrons, every chevron meaning five years' service. And the spirit of these men was terrible. They were raging, furious, fanatical, adoring the Emperor as a Mameluke does his prophet, ready to fall upon their own bayonets if their blood could serve him. If you had seen these fierce old veterans going into battle, with their flushed faces, their savage eyes, their furious yells, you would wonder that anything could stand against them. So high was the spirit of France at that time that every other spirit would have quailed before it; but these people, these English, had neither spirit nor soul, but only solid, immovable beef, against which we broke ourselves in vain. That was it, my friends! On the one side, poetry, gallantry, self-sacrifice – all that is beautiful and heroic. On the other side, beef. Our hopes, our ideals, our dreams – all were shattered on that terrible beef of Old England.

You have read how the Emperor gathered his forces, and then how he and I, with a hundred and thirty thousand veterans, hurried to the northern frontier and fell upon the Prussians and the English. On the 16th of June Ney held the English in play at Quatre Bras while we beat the Prussians at Ligny. It is not for me to say how far I contributed to that victory, but it is well known that the Hussars of Conflans covered themselves with glory. They fought well, these Prussians, and eight thousand of them were left upon the field. The Emperor thought that he had done with them, as he sent Marshal Grouchy with thirty-two thousand men to follow them up and to prevent their interfering with his plans. Then, with nearly eighty thousand men, he turned upon these 'Goddam' Englishmen. How much we had to avenge upon them, we Frenchmen – the guineas of Pitt, the hulks of Portsmouth, the invasion of Wellington, the perfidious victories of Nelson! At last the day of punishment seemed to have arisen.

Wellington had with him sixty-seven thousand men, but many of them were known to be Dutch and Belgian, who had no great desire to fight against us. Of good troops he had not fifty thousand. Finding himself in the presence of the Emperor in person with eighty thousand men, this Englishman was so paralysed with fear that he could neither move himself nor his army. You have seen the rabbit when the snake approaches. So stood the English upon the ridge of Waterloo. The night before, the Emperor, who had lost an aide-de-camp at Ligny, ordered me to join his staff, and I had left my Hussars to the charge of Major Victor. I know not which of us was the most grieved, they or I, that I should be called away upon the eve of battle; but an order is an order, and a good soldier can but shrug his shoulders and obey. With the Emperor I rode across the front of the enemy's position on the morning of the 18th, he looking at them through his glass and planning which was the shortest way to destroy them. Soult was at his elbow, and Ney and Foy and others who had fought the English in Portugal and Spain. 'Have a care, Sire,' said Soult, 'the English infantry is very solid.'

'You think them good soldiers because they have beaten you,' said the Emperor, and we younger men turned away our faces and smiled. But Ney and Foy were grave and serious. All the time the English line, chequered with red and blue and dotted with batteries, was drawn up silent and watchful within a long musket-shot of us. On the other side of the shallow valley our own people, having finished their soup, were assembling for the battle. It had rained very heavily; but at this moment the sun shone out and beat upon the French army, turning our brigades of cavalry into so many dazzling rivers of steel, and twinkling and sparkling on the innumerable bayonets of the infantry. At the sight of that splendid army, and the beauty and majesty of its appearance, I could contain myself no longer; but, rising in my stirrups, I waved my busby and cried, '*Vive l'Empereur !*' a shout which growled and roared and clattered from one end of the line to the other, while the horsemen waved their swords and the footmen held up their shakos upon their bayonets. The English remained petrified upon their ridge. They knew that their hour had come.

And so it would have come if at that moment the word had been given and the whole army had been permitted to advance. We had but to fall upon them and to sweep them from the face of the earth. To put aside all question of courage, we were the more numerous, the older soldiers, and the better led. But the Emperor desired to do all things in order, and he waited until the ground should be drier and harder, so that his artillery could manoeuvre. So three hours were wasted, and it was eleven o'clock before we saw Jerome Buonaparte's columns advance upon our left and heard the crash of the guns which told that the battle had begun. The loss of those three hours was our destruction. The attack upon the left was directed upon a farmhouse which was held by the English Guards, and we heard the three loud shouts of apprehension which the defenders were compelled to utter. They were still holding out, and D'Erlon's corps was advancing upon the right to engage another portion of the English line, when our attention was called away from the battle beneath our noses to a distant portion of the field of action.

The Emperor had been looking through his glass to the

extreme left of the English line, and now he turned suddenly to the Duke of Dalmatia, or Soult, as we soldiers preferred to call him.

'What is it, Marshal ?' said he.

We all followed the direction of his gaze, some raising our glasses, some shading our eyes. There was a thick wood over yonder, then a long, bare slope, and another wood beyond. Over this bare strip between the two woods there lay something dark, like the shadow of a moving cloud.

'I think they are cattle, Sire,' said Soult.

At that instant there came a quick twinkle from amid the dark shadow.

'It is Grouchy,' said the Emperor, and he lowered his glass. 'They are doubly lost, these English. I hold them in the hollow of my hand. They cannot escape me.'

He looked round, and his eyes fell upon me.

'Ah! here is the prince of messengers,' said he. 'Are you well mounted, Colonel Gerard ?'

I was riding my little Violette, the pride of the brigade. I said so.

'Then ride hard to Marshal Grouchy, whose troops you see over yonder. Tell him that he is to fall upon the left flank and rear of the English while I attack them in front. Together we shall crush them and not a man escape.'

I saluted and rode off without a word, my heart dancing with joy that such a mission should be mine. I looked at that long, solid line of red and blue looming through the smoke of the guns, and I shook my fist at it as I went. 'We shall crush them and not a man escape.' They were the Emperor's words, and it was I, Etienne Gerard, who was to turn them into deeds. I burned to reach the Marshal, and for an instant I thought of riding through the English left wing, as being the shortest cut. I have done bolder deeds and come out safely, but I reflected that if things went badly with me and I was taken or shot the message would be lost and the plans of the Emperor miscarry. I passed in front of the cavalry therefore, past the Chasseurs, the Lancers of the Guard, the Carabineers, the Horse Grenadiers and, lastly, my own little rascals, who followed me wistfully with their eyes. Beyond the cavalry the Old Guard was standing, twelve regiments of them, all veterans of many battles, sombre and severe, in long blue overcoats, and high bearskins from which the plumes had been removed. Each bore within the goatskin knapsack upon his back the blue and white parade uniform which they would use for their entry into Brussels next day. As I rode past them I reflected that these men had never been beaten, and, as I looked at their weather-beaten faces and their stern and silent bearing, I said to myself that they never would be beaten. Great heavens, how little could I foresee what a few more hours would bring!

On the right of the Old Guard were the Young Guard and the 6th Corps of Lobau, and then I passed Jacquinot's Lancers and Marbot's Hussars, who held the extreme flank of the line. All these troops knew nothing of the corps which was coming towards them through the wood, and their attention was taken up in watching the battle which raged upon their left. More than a hundred guns were thundering from each side, and the din was so great that of all the battles which I have fought I cannot recall more than half-a-dozen which were as noisy. I looked back over my shoulder, and there were two brigades of Cuirassiers, English and French, pouring down the hill together, with the sword-blades playing over them like summer lightning. How I longed to turn Violette, and to lead my Hussars into the thick of it! What a picture! Etienne Gerard with his back to the battle, and a fine cavalry action raging behind him. But duty is duty, so I rode past Marbot's vedettes and on in the direction of the wood, passing the village of Frishermont upon my left.

In front of me lay the great wood, called the Wood of Paris, consisting mostly of oak trees, with a few narrow paths leading through it. I halted and listened when I reached it; but out of its gloomy depths there came no blare of trumpet, no murmur of wheels, no tramp of horses to mark the advance of that great column which with my own eyes I had seen streaming towards it. The battle roared behind me, but in front all was as silent as that grave in which so many brave men would shortly sleep. The sunlight was cut off by the arches of leaves above my head, and a heavy damp smell rose from the sodden ground. For several miles I galloped at such a pace as few riders would care to go with roots below and branches above. Then, at last, for the first time I caught a glimpse of Grouchy's advance guard. Scattered parties of Hussars passed me on either side, but some distance off, among the trees. I heard the beating of a drum far away, and the low, dull murmur which an army makes upon the march. Any moment I might come upon the staff and deliver my message to Grouchy in person, for I knew well that on such a march a Marshal of France would certainly ride with the van of his army.

Suddenly the trees thinned in front of me, and I understood with delight that I was coming to the end of the wood, whence I could see the army and find the Marshal. Where the track comes out from amid the trees there is a small cabaret, where wood-cutters and waggoners drink their wine. Outside the door of this I reined up my horse for an instant while I took in the scene which was before me. Some few miles away I saw a second great forest, that of St Lambert, out of which the Emperor had seen the troops advancing. It was easy to see, however, why there had been so long a delay in their leaving one wood and reaching the other, because between the two ran the deep defile of the Lasnes, which had to be crossed. Sure enough, a long column of troops – horse, foot, and guns – was streaming down one side of it and swarming up the other, while the advance guard was already among the trees on either side of me. A battery of Horse Artillery was coming along the road, and I was about to gallop up to it and ask the officer in command if he could tell me where I should find the Marshal, when suddenly I observed that, though the gunners were dressed in blue, they had not the dolman trimmed with red brandenburgs as our own horse-gunners wear it. Amazed at the sight, I was looking at these soldiers to left and right when a hand touched my thigh, and there was the landlord, who had rushed from his inn.

'Madman!' he cried, 'why are you here? What are you doing?'

'I am seeking Marshal Grouchy.'

'You are in the heart of the Prussian army. Turn and fly!'

'Impossible; this is Grouchy's corps.'

'How do you know?'

'Because the Emperor has said it.'

'Then the Emperor has made a terrible mistake! I tell you that a patrol of Silesian Hussars has this instant left me. Did you not see them in the wood?'

'I saw Hussars.'

'They are the enemy.'

'Where is Grouchy?'

'He is behind. They have passed him.'

'Then how can I go back? If I go forward I may see him yet. I must obey my orders and find him wherever he is.'

The man reflected for an instant.

'Quick! quick!' he cried, seizing my bridle. 'Do what I say and you may yet escape. They have not observed you yet. Come with me and I will hide you until they pass.'

Behind his house there was a low stable, and into this he thrust Violette. Then he half led and half dragged me into the kitchen of the inn. It was a bare, brick-floored room. A stout, red-faced woman was cooking cutlets at the fire.

'What's the matter now?' she asked, looking with a frown from me to the innkeeper. 'Who is this you have brought in?'

'It is a French officer, Marie. We cannot let the Prussians take him.'

'Why not?'

'Why not? Sacred name of a dog, was I not myself a soldier of Napoleon? Did I not win a musket of honour among the Vélites of the Guard? Shall I see a comrade taken before my eyes? Marie, we must save him.'

But the lady looked at me with most unfriendly eyes.

'Pierre Charras,' she said, 'you will not rest until you have your house burned over your head. Do you not understand, you blockhead, that if you fought for Napoleon it was because Napoleon ruled Belgium? He does so no longer. The Prussians are our allies and this is our enemy. I will have no Frenchman in this house. Give him up!'

The innkeeper scratched his head and looked at me in despair, but it was very evident to me that it was neither for France nor for Belgium that this woman cared, but that it was the safety of her own house that was nearest her heart.

'Madame,' said I, with all the dignity and assurance I could command, 'the Emperor is defeating the English and the French army will be here before evening. If you have used me well you will be rewarded, and if you have denounced me you will be punished and your house will certainly be burned by the provost-marshal.'

She was shaken by this, and I hastened to complete my victory by other methods.

'Surely,' said I, 'it is impossible that anyone so beautiful can also be hard-hearted? You will not refuse me the refuge which I need.'

She looked at my whiskers and I saw that she was softened. I took her hand, and in two minutes we were on such terms that her husband swore roundly that he would give me up himself if I pressed the matter farther.

'Besides, the road is full of Prussians,' he cried. 'Quick! quick! into the loft!'

'Quick! quick! into the loft!' echoed his wife, and together they hurried me towards a ladder which led to a trap-door in the ceiling. There was a loud knocking at the door, so you can think that it was not long before my spurs went twinkling through the hole and the board was dropped behind me. An instant later I heard the voices of the Germans in the rooms below me.

The place in which I found myself was a single long attic, the ceiling of which was formed by the roof of the house. It ran over the whole of one side of the inn, and through the cracks in the flooring I could look down either upon the kitchen, the sitting-room, or the bar at my pleasure. There were no windows, but the place was in the last stage of disrepair, and several missing slates upon the roof gave me light and the means of observation. The place was heaped with lumber – fodder at one end and a huge pile of empty bottles at the other. There was no door or window save the hole through which I had come up.

I sat upon the heap of hay for a few minutes to steady myself and to think out my plans. It was very serious that the Prussians should arrive upon the field of battle earlier than our reserves, but there appeared to be only one corps of them, and a corps more or less makes little difference to such a man as the Emperor. He could afford to give the English all this and beat them still. The best way in which I could serve him, since Grouchy was behind, was to wait here until they were past, and then to resume my journey, to see the Marshal, and to give him his orders. If he advanced upon the rear of the English instead of following the Prussians all would be well. The fate of France depended upon my judgement and my nerve. It was not the first time, my friends, as you are well aware, and you know the reasons that I had to trust that neither nerve nor judgement would ever fail me. Certainly, the Emperor had chosen the right man for his mission. 'The prince of messengers' he had called me. I would earn my title.

It was clear that I could do nothing until the Prussians had passed, so I spent my time in observing them. I have no love for these people, but I am compelled to say that they kept excellent discipline, for not a man of them entered the inn, though their lips were caked with dust and they were ready to drop with fatigue. Those who had knocked at the door were bearing an insensible comrade, and having left him they returned at once to the ranks. Several others were carried in the same fashion and laid in the kitchen, while a young surgeon, little more than a boy, remained behind in charge of them. Having observed them through the cracks in the floor, I next turned my attention to the holes in the roof, from which I had an excellent view of all that was passing outside. The Prussian corps was still streaming past. It was easy to see that they had made a terrible march and had little food, for the faces of the men were ghastly, and they were plastered from head to foot with mud from their falls upon the foul and slippery roads. Yet, spent as they were, their spirit was excellent, and they pushed and hauled at the gun-carriages when the wheels sank up to the axles in the mire, and the weary horses were floundering knee-deep unable to draw them through. The officers rode up and down the column encouraging the more active with words of praise, and the laggards with blows from the flat of their swords. All the time from over the wood in front of them there came the tremendous roar of the battle, as if all the rivers on earth had united in one gigantic cataract, booming and crashing in a mighty fall. Like the spray of the cataract was the long veil of smoke which rose high over the trees. The officers pointed to it with their swords, and with hoarse cries from their parched lips the mud-stained men pushed onwards to the battle. For an hour I watched them pass, and I reflected that their vanguard must have come into touch with Marbot's vedettes and that the Emperor knew already of their coming. 'You are going very fast up the road, my friends, but you will come down it a great deal faster,' said I to myself, and I consoled myself with the thought.

But an adventure came to break the monotony of this long wait. I was seated beside my loophole and congratulating myself that the corps was nearly past, and that the road would soon be clear for my journey, when suddenly I heard a loud altercation break out in French in the kitchen.

'You shall not go!' cried a woman's voice.

'I tell you that I will!' said a man's, and there was a sound of scuffling.

In an instant I had my eye to the crack in the floor. There was my stout lady, like a faithful watch-dog, at the bottom of the ladder; while the young German surgeon, white with anger, was endeavouring to come up it. Several of the German soldiers who had recovered from their prostration were sitting about on the kitchen floor and watching the quarrel with stolid, but attentive, faces. The landlord was nowhere to be seen.

'There is no liquor there,' said the woman.

'I do not want liquor; I want hay or straw for these men to lie upon. Why should they lie on the bricks when there is straw overhead ?'

'There is no straw.'

'What is up there ?'

'Empty bottles.'

'Nothing else ?'

'No.'

For a moment it looked as if the surgeon would abandon his intention, but one of the soldiers pointed up to the ceiling. I gathered from what I could understand of his words that he could see the straw sticking out between the planks. In vain the woman protested. Two of the soldiers were able to get upon their feet and to drag her aside, while the young surgeon ran up the ladder, pushed open the trap-door, and climbed into the loft. As he swung the door back I slipped behind it, but as luck would have it he shut it again behind him, and there we were left standing face to face.

Never have I seen a more astonished young man.

'A French officer!' he gasped.

'Hush!' said I. 'Hush! Not a word above a whisper.' I had drawn my sword.

'I am not a combatant,' he said; 'I am a doctor. Why do you threaten me with your sword ? I am not armed.'

'I do not wish to hurt you, but I must protect myself. I am in hiding here.'

'A spy!'

'A spy does not wear such a uniform as this, nor do you find spies on the staff of an army. I rode by mistake into the heart of this Prussian corps, and I concealed myself here in the hope of escaping when they are past. I will not hurt you if you do not hurt me, but if you do not swear that you will be silent as to my presence you will never go down alive from this attic.'

'You can put up your sword, sir,' said the surgeon, and I saw a friendly twinkle in his eyes. 'I am a Pole by birth, and have no ill feeling to you or your people. I will do my best for my patients, but I will do no more. Capturing Hussars is not one of the duties of a surgeon. With your permission I will now descend with this truss of hay to make a couch for these poor fellows below.'

I had intended to exact an oath from him, but it is my experience that if a man will not speak the truth he will not swear the truth, so I said no more. The surgeon opened the trap-door, threw out enough hay for his purpose, and then descended the ladder, letting down the door behind him. I watched him anxiously when he rejoined his patients, and so did my good friend the landlady, but he said nothing and busied himself with the needs of the soldiers.

By this time I was sure that the last of the army corps was past, and I went to my loophole confident [that I should find the coast clear, save, perhaps, for a few stragglers, whom I could disregard. The first corps was indeed past, and I could see the last files of the infantry disappearing into the wood; but you can imagine my disappointment when out of the Forest of St Lambert I saw a second corps emerging, as numerous as the first. There could be no doubt that the whole Prussian army, which we thought we had destroyed at Ligny, was about to throw itself upon our right wing while Marshal Grouchy had been coaxed away upon some fool's errand. The roar of guns, much nearer than before, told me that the Prussian batteries which had passed me were already in action. Imagine my terrible position! Hour after hour was passing; the sun was sinking towards the west. And yet this cursed inn, in which I lay hid, was like a little island amid a rushing stream of furious Prussians. It was all important that I should reach Marshal Grouchy, and yet I could not show my nose without being made prisoner. You can think how I cursed and tore my hair. How little do we know what is in store for us! Even while I raged against my ill-fortune, that same fortune was reserving me for a far higher task than to carry a message to Grouchy – a task which could not have been mine had I not been held tight in that little inn on the edge of the Forest of Paris.

Two Prussian corps had passed and a third was coming up, when I heard a great fuss and the sound of several voices in the sitting-room. By altering my position I was able to look down and see what was going on.

Two Prussian generals were beneath me, their heads bent over a map which lay upon the table. Several aides-de-camp and staff officers stood round in silence. Of the two generals one was a fierce old man, white-haired and wrinkled, with a ragged, grizzled moustache and a voice like the bark of a hound. The other was younger, but long-faced and solemn. He measured distances upon the map with the air of a student, while his companion stamped and fumed and cursed like a corporal of Hussars. It was strange to see the old man so fiery and the young one so reserved. I could not understand all that they said, but I was very sure about their general meaning.

'I tell you we must push on and ever on!' cried the old fellow, with a furious German oath. 'I promised Wellington that I would be there with the whole army even if I had to be strapped to my horse. Bülow's corps is in action, and Zeithen's shall support it with every man and gun. Forwards, Gneisenau, forwards!'

The other shook his head.

'You must remember, your Excellency, that if the English are beaten they will make for the coast. What will your position be then, with Grouchy between you and the Rhine?'

'We shall beat them, Gneisenau; the Duke and I will grind them to powder between us. Push on, I say! The whole war will be ended in one blow. Bring Pirsch up, and we can throw sixty thousand men into the scale while Thielmann holds Grouchy beyond Wavre.'

Gneisenau shrugged his shoulders, but at that instant an orderly appeared at the door.

'An aide-de-camp from the Duke of Wellington,' said he.

'Ha, ha!' cried the old man; 'let us hear what he has to say.'

An English officer, with mud and blood all over his scarlet jacket, staggered into the room. A crimson-stained handkerchief was knotted round his arm, and he held the table to keep himself from falling.

'My message is to Marshal Blücher,' says he.

'I am Marshal Blücher. Go on! go on!' cried the impatient old man.

'The Duke bade me to tell you, sir, that the British army can hold its own, and that he has no fears for the result. The French cavalry has been destroyed, two of their divisions of infantry have ceased to exist, and only the Guard is in reserve. If you give us a vigorous support the defeat will be changed to absolute rout and—' His knees gave way under him, and he fell in a heap upon the floor.

'Enough! enough!' cried Blücher. 'Gneisenau, send an aide-de-camp to Wellington and tell him to rely upon me to the full. Come on, gentlemen, we have our work to do!' He bustled eagerly out of the room, with all his staff clanking behind him, while two orderlies carried the English messenger to the care of the surgeon.

Gneisenau, the Chief of the Staff, had lingered behind for an instant, and he laid his hand upon one of the aides-de-camp. The fellow had attracted my attention, for I have always a quick eye for a fine man. He was tall and slender, the very model of a horseman; indeed, there was something in his appearance which made it not unlike my own. His face was dark and as keen as that of a hawk, with fierce black eyes under thick, shaggy brows, and a moustache which would have put him in the crack squadron of my Hussars. He wore a green coat with white facings, and a horsehair helmet – a Dragoon, as I conjectured, and as dashing a cavalier as one would wish to have at the end of one's sword-point.

'A word with you, Count Stein,' said Gneisenau. 'If the enemy are routed, but if the Emperor escapes, he will rally another army, and all will have to be done again. But if we can get the Emperor, then the war is indeed ended. It is worth a great effort and a great risk for such an object as that.'

The young Dragoon said nothing, but he listened attentively.

'Suppose the Duke of Wellington's words should prove to be correct, and the French army should be driven in utter rout from the field, the Emperor will certainly take the road back through Genappe and Charleroi as being the shortest to the frontier. We can imagine that his horses will be fleet, and that the fugitives will make way for him. Our cavalry will follow the rear of the beaten army, but the Emperor will be far away at the front of the throng.'

The young Dragoon inclined his head.

'To you, Count Stein, I commit the Emperor. If you take him your name will live in history. You have the reputation of being the hardest rider in our army. Do you choose such comrades as you may select – ten or a dozen should be enough. You are not to engage in the battle, nor are you to follow the general pursuit, but you are to ride clear of the crowd, reserving your energies for a nobler end. Do you understand me?'

Again the Dragoon inclined his head. This silence impressed me. I felt that he was indeed a dangerous man.

'Then I leave the details in your own hands. Strike at no one except the highest. You cannot mistake the Imperial carriage, nor can you fail to recognise the figure of the Emperor. Now I must follow the Marshal. Adieu! If ever I see you again I trust that it will be to congratulate you upon a deed which will ring through Europe.'

The Dragoon saluted, and Gneisenau hurried from the room. The young officer stood in deep thought for a few moments. Then he followed the Chief of the Staff. I looked with curiosity from my loophole to see what his next proceeding would be. His horse, a fine, strong chestnut with two white stockings, was fastened to the rail of the inn. He sprang into the saddle, and, riding to intercept a column of cavalry which was passing, he spoke to an officer at the head of the leading regiment. Presently, after some talk, I saw two Hussars – it was a Hussar regiment – drop out of the ranks and take up their position beside Count Stein. The next regiment was also stopped, and two Lancers were added to his escort. The next furnished him with two Dragoons, and the next with two Cuirassiers. Then he drew his little group of horsemen aside, and he gathered them round him, explaining to them what they had to do. Finally the nine soldiers rode off together and disappeared into the Wood of Paris.

I need not tell you, my friends, what all this portended. Indeed, he had acted exactly as I should have done in his place. From each colonel he had demanded the two best horsemen in the regiment, and so he had assembled a band who might expect to catch whatever they should follow. Heaven help the Emperor if, without an escort, he should find them on his track!

And I, dear friends – imagine the fever, the ferment, the madness, of my mind! All thought of Grouchy had passed away. No guns were to be heard to the east. He could not be near. If he should come he would not now be in time to alter the event of the day. The sun was already low in the sky and there could not be more than two or three hours of daylight. My mission might be dismissed as useless. But here was another mission, more pressing, more immediate, a mission which meant the safety, and perhaps the life, of the Emperor. At all costs, through every danger, I must get back to his side. But how was I to do it? The whole Prussian army was now between me and the French lines. They blocked every road, but they could not block the path of duty when Etienne Gerard sees it lie before him. I could not wait longer. I must be gone.

There was but the one opening to the loft, and so it was only down the ladder that I could descend. I looked into the kitchen, and I found that the young surgeon was still there. In a chair sat the wounded English aide-de-camp, and on the straw lay two Prussian soldiers in the last stage of exhaustion. The others had all recovered and been sent on. These were my enemies, and I must pass through them in order to gain my horse. From the surgeon I had nothing to fear; the Englishman was wounded, and his sword stood with his cloak in a corner; the two Germans were half insensible, and their muskets were not beside them. What could be simpler? I opened the trap-door, slipped down the ladder, and appeared in the midst of them, my sword drawn in my hand.

What a picture of surprise! The surgeon, of course, knew all, but to the Englishman and the two Germans it must have seemed that the god of war in person had descended from the skies. With my appearance, with my figure, with my silver and grey uniform, and with that gleaming sword in my hand, I must indeed have been a sight worth seeing. The two Germans lay petrified, with staring eyes. The English officer half rose, but sat down again from weakness, his mouth open and his hand on the back of his chair.

'What the deuce!' he kept on repeating, 'what the deuce!'

'Pray do not move,' said I; 'I will hurt no one, but woe to the man who lays hands upon me to stop me. You have nothing to fear if you leave me alone, and nothing to hope if you try to hinder me. I am Colonel Etienne Gerard, of the Hussars of Conflans.'

'The deuce!' said the Englishman. 'You are the man that killed the fox.' A terrible scowl had darkened his face. The jealousy of sportsmen is a base passion. He hated me, this Englishman, because I had been before him in transfixing the animal. How different are our natures! Had I seen him do such a deed I would have embraced him with cries of joy. But there was no time for argument.

'I regret it, sir,' said I; 'but you have a cloak here and I must take it.'

He tried to rise from his chair and reach his sword, but I got between him and the corner where it lay.

'If there is anything in the pockets—'

'A case,' said he.

'I would not rob you,' said I; and raising the coat I took from the pockets a silver flask, a square wooden case, and a field-glass. All these I handed to him. The wretch opened the case, took out a pistol, and pointed it straight at my head.

'Now, my fine fellow,' said he, 'put down your sword and give yourself up.'

I was so astonished at this infamous action that I stood petrified before him. I tried to speak to him of honour and gratitude, but I saw his eyes fix and harden over the pistol.

'Enough talk!' said he. 'Drop it!'

Could I endure such a humiliation? Death were better than to be disarmed in such a fashion. The word 'Fire!' was on my lips when in an instant the Englishman vanished from before my face, and in his place was a great pile of hay, with a red-coated arm and two Hessian boots waving and kicking in the heart of it. Oh, the gallant landlady! It was my whiskers that had saved me.

'Fly, soldier, fly!' she cried, and she heaped fresh trusses of hay from the floor on to the struggling Englishman. In an instant I was out in the courtyard, had led Violette from her stable, and was on her back. A pistol bullet whizzed past my shoulder from the window, and I saw a furious face looking out at me. I smiled my contempt and spurred out into the road. The last of the Prussians had passed, and both my road and my duty lay clear before me. If France won, all was well. If France lost, then on me and on my little mare depended that which was more than victory or defeat – the safety and the life of the Emperor. 'On, Etienne, on!' I cried. 'Of all your noble exploits, the greatest, even if it be the last, lies now before you!'

2 The story of the nine Prussian horsemen

I told you when last we met, my friends, of the important mission from the Emperor to Marshal Grouchy, which failed through no fault of my own, and I described to you how during a long afternoon I was shut up in the attic of a country inn, and was prevented from coming out because the Prussians were all around me. You will remember also how I overheard the Chief of the Prussian Staff give his instructions to Count Stein, and so learned the dangerous plan which was on foot to kill or capture the Emperor in the event of a French defeat. At first I could not have believed in such a thing, but since the guns had thundered all day, and since the sound had made no advance in my direction, it was evident that the English had at least held their own and beaten off all our attacks.

I have said that it was a fight that day between the soul of France and the beef of England, but it must be confessed that we found the beef was very tough. It was clear that if the Emperor could not defeat the English when alone, then it might, indeed, go hard with him now that sixty thousand of these cursed Prussians were swarming on his flank. In any case, with this secret in my possession, my place was by his side.

I had made my way out of the inn in the dashing manner which I have described to you when last we met, and I left the English aide-de-camp shaking his foolish fist out of the window. I could not but laugh as I looked back at him, for his angry red face was framed and frilled with hay. Once out on the road I stood erect in my stirrups, and I put on the handsome black riding-coat, lined with red, which had belonged to him. It fell to the top of my high boots, and covered my tell-tale uniform completely. As to my busby, there are many such in the German service, and there was no reason why it should attract attention. So long as no one spoke to me there was no reason why I should not ride through the whole of the Prussian army; but though I understood German, for I had many friends among the German ladies during the pleasant years that I fought all over that country, still I spoke it with a pretty Parisian accent which could not be confounded with their rough, unmusical speech. I knew that this quality of my accent would attract attention, but I could only hope and pray that I would be permitted to go my way in silence.

The Forest of Paris was so large that it was useless to think of going round it, and so I took my courage in both hands and galloped on down the road in the track of the Prussian army. It was not hard to trace it, for it was rutted two feet deep by the gunwheels and the caissons. Soon I found a fringe of wounded men, Prussians and French, on each side of it, where Bülow's advance had come into touch with Marbot's Hussars. One old man with a long white beard, a surgeon, I suppose, shouted at me, and ran after me still shouting, but I never turned my head and took no notice of him save to spur on faster. I heard his shouts long after I had lost sight of him among the trees.

Presently I came up with the Prussian reserves. The infantry were leaning on their muskets or lying exhausted on the wet ground, and the officers stood in groups listening to the mighty roar of the battle and discussing the reports which came from the front. I hurried past at the top of my speed, but one of them rushed out and stood in my path with his hand up as a signal to me to stop. Five thousand Prussian eyes were turned upon me. There was a moment! You turn pale, my friends, at the thought of it. Think how every hair upon me stood on end. But never for one instant did my wits or my courage desert me. 'General Blücher!' I cried. Was it not my guardian angel who whispered the words in my ear? The Prussian sprang from my path, saluted and pointed forwards. They are well disciplined, these Prussians, and who was he that he should dare to stop the officer who bore a message to the general? It was a talisman that would pass me out of every danger, and my heart sang within me at the thought. So elated was I that I no longer waited to be asked, but as I rode through the army I shouted to right and left, 'General Blücher! General Blücher!' and every man pointed me onwards and cleared a path to let me pass. There are times when the most supreme impudence is the highest wisdom. But discretion must also be used, and I must admit that I became indiscreet. For as I rode upon my way, ever nearer to the fighting line, a Prussian officer of Uhlans gripped my bridle and pointed to a group of men who stood near a burning farm. 'There is Marshal Blücher. Deliver your message!' said he, and sure enough my terrible old grey-whiskered veteran was there within a pistol shot, his eyes turned in my direction.

But the good guardian angel did not desert me. Quick as a flash there came into my memory the name of the general who commanded the advance of the Prussians. 'General Bülow!' I cried. The Uhlan let go my bridle. 'General Bülow! General Bülow!' I shouted as every stride of the dear little mare took me nearer my own people. Through the burning village of Plancenoit I galloped, spurred my way between two columns of Prussian infantry, sprang over a hedge, cut down a Silesian Hussar who flung himself before me, and an instant afterwards, with my coat flying open to show the uniform below, I passed through the open files of the tenth of the line and was back in the heart of Lobau's corps once more. Outnumbered and outflanked, they were being slowly driven in by the pressure of the Prussian advance. I galloped onwards, anxious only to find myself by the Emperor's side.

But a sight lay before me which held me fast as though I had been turned into some noble equestrian statue. I could not move, I could scarce breathe, as I gazed upon it. There was a mound over which my path lay, and as I came out on the top of it I looked down the long shallow valley of Waterloo. I had left it with two great armies on either side and a clear field between them. Now there were but long, ragged fringes of broken and exhausted regiments upon the two ridges, but a real army of dead and wounded lay between. For two miles in length and half a mile across the ground was strewed and heaped with them. But slaughter was no new sight to me, and it was not that which held me spellbound. It was that up the long slope of the British position was moving a walking forest – black, tossing, waving, unbroken. Did I not know the bearskins of the Guard? And did I not also know, did not my soldier's instinct tell me, that it was the last reserve of France; that the Emperor, like a desperate gamester, was staking all upon his last card? Up they went and up – grand, solid, unbreakable, scourged with musketry, riddled with grape, flowing onwards in a black, heavy tide, which lapped over the British batteries. With my glass I could see the English gunners throw themselves under their pieces or run to the rear. On rolled the crest of the bearskins, and then, with a crash which was swept across to my ears, they met the British infantry. A minute passed, and another, and another. My heart was in my mouth. They swayed back and forwards; they no longer advanced; they were held. Great Heaven! was it possible that they were breaking? One black dot ran down the hill, then two, then four, then ten, then a great, scattered, struggling mass, halting, breaking, halting, and at last shredding out and rushing madly downwards. 'The Guard is beaten! The Guard is beaten!' From all around me I heard the cry. Along the whole line the infantry turned their faces and the gunners flinched from their guns.

'The Old Guard is beaten! The Guard retreats!' An officer with a livid face passed me yelling out these words of woe. 'Save yourselves! Save yourselves! You are betrayed!' cried another. 'Save yourselves! Save yourselves!' Men were rushing madly to the rear, blundering and jumping like frightened sheep. Cries and screams rose from all around me. And at that moment, as I looked at the British position, I saw what I can never forget. A single horseman stood out black and clear upon the ridge against the last red angry glow of the setting sun. So dark, so motionless against that grim light, he might have been the very spirit of Battle brooding over that terrible valley. As I gazed he raised his hat high in the air, and at the signal, with a low, deep roar like a breaking wave, the whole British army flooded over their ridge and came rolling down into the valley. Long steel-fringed lines of red and blue, sweeping waves of cavalry, horse batteries rattling and bounding – down they came on to our crumbling ranks. It was over. A yell of agony, the agony of brave men who see no hope, rose from one flank to the other, and in an instant the whole of that noble army was swept in a wild, terror-stricken crowd from the field. Even now, dear friends, I cannot, as you see, speak of that dreadful moment with a dry eye or with a steady voice.

At first I was carried away in that wild rush, whirled off

like a straw in a flooded gutter. But, suddenly, what should I see amongst the mixed regiments in front of me but a group of stern horsemen, in silver and grey, with a broken and tattered standard held aloft in the heart of them! Not all the might of England and of Prussia could break the Hussars of Conflans. But when I joined them it made my heart bleed to see them. The major, seven captains, and five hundred men were left upon the field. Young Captain Sabbatier was in command, and when I asked him where were the five missing squadrons he pointed back and answered: 'You will find them round one of those British squares.' Men and horses were at their last gasp, caked with sweat and dirt, their black tongues hanging out from their lips; but it made me thrill with pride to see how that shattered remnant still rode knee to knee, with every man, from the boy trumpeter to the farrier-sergeant, in his own proper place. Would that I could have brought them on with me as an escort for the Emperor! In the heart of the Hussars of Conflans he would be safe indeed. But the horses were too spent to trot. I left them behind me with orders to rally upon the farmhouse of St Aunay, where we had camped two nights before. For my own part I forced my horse through the throng in search of the Emperor.

There were things which I saw then, as I pressed through that dreadful crowd, which can never be banished from my mind. In evil dreams there comes back to me the memory of that flowing stream of livid, staring, screaming faces upon which I looked down. It was a nightmare. In victory one does not understand the horror of war. It is only in the cold chill of defeat that it is brought home to you. I remember an old Grenadier of the Guard lying at the side of the road with his broken leg doubled at a right angle. 'Comrades, comrades, keep off my leg!' he cried, but they tripped and stumbled over him all the same. In front of me rode a Lancer officer without his coat. His arm had just been taken off in the ambulance. The bandages had fallen. It was horrible. Two gunners tried to drive through with their gun. A Chasseur raised his musket and shot one of them through the head. I saw a major of Cuirassiers draw his two holster pistols and shoot first his horse and then himself. Beside the road a man in a blue coat was raging and raving like a madman. His face was black with powder, his clothes were torn, one epaulette was gone, the other hung dangling over his breast. Only when I came close to him did I recognize that it was Marshal Ney. He howled at the flying troops and his voice was hardly human. Then he raised the stump of his sword – it was broken three inches from the hilt. 'Come and see how a Marshal of France can die!' he cried. Gladly would I have gone with him, but my duty lay elsewhere. He did not, as you know, find the death he sought, but he met it a few weeks later in cold blood at the hands of his enemies.

There is an old proverb that in attack the French are more than men, in defeat they are less than women. I knew that it was true that day. But even in that rout I saw things which I can tell with pride. Through the fields which skirt the road moved Cambronne's three reserve battalions of the Guard, the cream of our army. They walked slowly in square, their colours waving over the sombre line of the bearskins. All around them raged the English cavalry and the black Lancers of Brunswick, wave after wave thundering up, breaking with a crash, and recoiling in ruin. When last I saw them the English guns, six at a time, were smashing grape-shot through their ranks, and the English infantry were closing in upon three sides and pouring volleys into them; but still, like a noble lion with fierce hounds clinging to its flanks, the glorious remnant of the Guard, marching slowly, halting, closing up, dressing, moved majestically from their last battle. Behind them the Guards' battery of twelve-pounders was drawn up upon the ridge. Every gunner was in his place, but no gun fired. 'Why do you not fire?' I asked the colonel as I passed. 'Our powder is finished.' 'Then why not retire?' 'Our appearance may hold them back for a little. We must give the Emperor time to escape.' Such were the soldiers of France.

Behind this screen of brave men the others took their breath, and then went on in less desperate fashion. They had broken away from the road, and all over the country-side in the twilight I could see the timid, scattered, frightened crowd who ten hours before had formed the finest army that ever went down to battle. I with my splendid mare was soon able to get clear of the throng, and just after I passed Genappe I overtook the Emperor with the remains of his Staff. Soult was with him still, and so were Drouot, Lobau, and Bertrand, with five Chasseurs of the Guard, their horses hardly able to move. The night was falling, and the Emperor's haggard face gleamed white through the gloom as he turned it towards me.

'Who is that?' he asked.

'It is Colonel Gerard,' said Soult.

'Have you seen Marshal Grouchy?'

'No, Sire. The Prussians were between.'

'It does not matter. Nothing matters now. Soult, I will go back.'

He tried to turn his horse, but Bertrand seized his bridle. 'Ah, Sire,' said Soult, 'the enemy has had good fortune enough already.' They forced him on among them. He rode in silence with his chin upon his breast, the greatest and the saddest of men. Far away behind us those remorseless guns were still roaring. Sometimes out of the darkness would come shrieks and screams and the low thunder of galloping hoofs. At the sound we would spur our horses and hasten onwards through the scattered troops. At last, after riding all night in the clear moonlight, we found that we had left both pursued and pursuers behind. By the time we passed over the bridge at Charleroi the dawn was breaking. What a company of spectres we looked in that cold, clear, searching light, the Emperor with his face of wax, Soult blotched with powder, Lobau dabbled with blood! But we rode more easily now and had ceased to glance over our shoulders, for Waterloo was more than thirty miles behind us. One of the Emperor's carriages had been picked up at Charleroi, and we halted now on the other side of the Sambre, and dismounted from our horses.

You will ask me why it was that during all this time I had

said nothing of that which was nearest my heart, the need for guarding the Emperor. As a fact, I had tried to speak of it both to Soult and to Lobau, but their minds were so overwhelmed with the disaster and so distracted by the pressing needs of the moment that it was impossible to make them understand how urgent was my message. Besides, during this long flight we had always had numbers of French fugitives beside us on the road, and, however demoralised they might be, we had nothing to fear from the attack of nine men. But now, as we stood round the Emperor's carriage in the early morning, I observed with anxiety that not a single French soldier was to be seen upon the long, white road behind us. We had outstripped the army. I looked round to see what means of defence were left to us. The horses of the Chasseurs of the Guard had broken down, and only one of them, a grey-whiskered sergeant, remained. There were Soult, Lobau, and Bertrand; but, for all their talents, I had rather, when it came to hard knocks, have a single quartermaster-sergeant of Hussars at my side than the three of them put together. There remained the Emperor himself, the coachman, and a valet of the household who had joined us at Charleroi – eight all told; but of the eight only two, the Chasseur and I, were fighting soldiers who could be depended upon at a pinch. A chill came over me as I reflected how utterly helpless we were. At that moment I raised my eyes, and there were the nine Prussian horsemen coming over the hill.

On either side of the road at this point are long stretches of rolling plain, part of it yellow with corn and part of it rich grass land watered by the Sambre. To the south of us was a low ridge, over which was the road to France. Along this road the little group of cavalry was riding. So well had Count Stein obeyed his instructions that he had struck far to the south of us in his determination to get ahead of the Emperor. Now he was riding from the direction in which we were going – the last in which we could expect an enemy. When I caught that first glimpse of them they were still half a mile away.

'Sire!' I cried, 'the Prussians!'

They all started and stared. It was the Emperor who broke the silence.

'Who says they are Prussians?'

'I do, Sire – I, Etienne Gerard!'

Unpleasant news always made the Emperor furious against the man who broke it. He railed at me now in the rasping, croaking, Corsican voice which only made itself heard when he had lost his self-control.

'You were always a buffoon,' he cried. 'What do you mean, you numskull, by saying that they are Prussians? How could Prussians be coming from the direction of France? You have lost any wits that you ever possessed.'

His words cut me like a whip, and yet we all felt towards the Emperor as an old dog does to its master. His kick is soon forgotten and forgiven. I would not argue or justify myself. At the first glance I had seen the two white stockings on the forelegs of the leading horse, and I knew well that Count Stein was on its back. For an instant the nine horsemen had halted and surveyed us. Now they put spurs to their horses, and with a yell of triumph they galloped down the road. They had recognized that their prey was in their power.

At that swift advance all doubt had vanished. 'By heavens, Sire, it is indeed the Prussians!' cried Soult. Lobau and Bertrand ran about the road like two frightened hens. The sergeant of Chasseurs drew his sabre with a volley of curses. The coachman and the valet cried and wrung their hands. Napoleon stood with a frozen face, one foot on the step of the carriage. And I – ah, my friends, I was magnificent! What words can I use to do justice to my own bearing at that supreme instant of my life! So coldly alert, so deadly cool, so clear in brain and ready in hand. He had called me a numskull and a buffoon. How quick and how noble was my revenge! When his own wits failed him, it was Etienne Gerard who supplied the want.

To fight was absurd; to fly was ridiculous. The Emperor was stout, and weary to death. At the best he was never a good rider. How could he fly from these, the picked men of an army? The best horseman in Prussia was among them. But I was the best horseman in France. I, and only I, could hold my own with them. If they were on *my* track instead of the Emperor's, all might still be well. These were the thoughts which flashed so swiftly through my mind that in an instant I had sprung from the first idea to the final conclusion. Another instant carried me from the final conclusion to prompt and vigorous action. I rushed to the side of the Emperor, who stood petrified, with the carriage between him and our enemies. 'Your coat, Sire! your hat!' I cried. I dragged them off him. Never had he been so hustled in his life. In an instant I had them on and had thrust him into the carriage. The next I had sprung on to his famous white Arab and had ridden clear of the group upon the road.

You have already divined my plan; but you may well ask how could I hope to pass myself off as the Emperor. My figure is as you still see it, and his was never beautiful, for he was both short and stout. But a man's height is not remarked when he is in the saddle, and for the rest one had but to sit forward on the horse and round one's back and carry oneself like a sack of flour. I wore the little cocked hat and the loose grey coat with the silver star which was known to every child from one end of Europe to the other. Beneath me was the Emperor's own white charger. It was complete.

Already as I rode clear the Prussians were within two hundred yards of us. I made a gesture of terror and despair with my hands, and I sprang my horse over the bank which lined the road. It was enough. A yell of exultation and of furious hatred broke from the Prussians. It was the howl of starving wolves who scent their prey. I spurred my horse over the meadow-land and looked back under my arm as I rode. Oh, the glorious moment when one after the other I saw eight horsemen come over the bank at my heels! Only one had stayed behind, and I heard shouting and the sounds of a struggle. I remembered my old sergeant of Chasseurs, and I was sure that number nine would trouble us no more.

The road was clear, and the Emperor free to continue his journey.

But now I had to think of myself. If I were overtaken the Prussians would certainly make short work of me in their disappointment. If it were so – if I lost my life – I should still have sold it at a glorious price. But I had hopes that I might shake them off. With ordinary horsemen upon ordinary horses I should still have had no difficulty in doing so, but here both steeds and riders were of the best. It was a grand creature that I rode, but it was weary with its long night's work, and the Emperor was one of those riders who do not know how to manage a horse. He had little thought for them, and a heavy hand upon their mouths. On the other hand Stein and his men had come both far and fast. The race was a fair one.

So quick had been my impulse, and so rapidly had I acted upon it, that I had not thought enough of my own safety. Had I done so in the first instance I should, of course, have ridden straight back the way we had come, for so I should have met our own people. But I was off the road and had galloped a mile over the plain before this occurred to me. Then when I looked back I saw that the Prussians had spread out into a long line, so as to head me off from the Charleroi road. I could not turn back, but at least I could edge towards the north. I knew that the whole face of the country was covered with our flying troops, and that sooner or later I must come upon some of them.

But one thing I had forgotten – the Sambre. In my excitement I never gave it a thought until I saw it deep and broad, gleaming in the morning sunlight. It barred my path, and the Prussians howled behind me. I galloped to the brink, but the horse refused the plunge. I spurred him, but the bank was high and the stream deep. He shrank back trembling and snorting. The yells of triumph were louder every instant. I turned and rode for my life down the river bank. It formed a loop at this part, and I must get across somehow, for my retreat was blocked. Suddenly a thrill of hope ran through me, for I saw a house on my side of the stream and another on the farther bank. Where there are two such houses it usually means that there is a ford between them. A sloping path led to the brink, and I urged my horse down it. On he went, the water up to the saddle, the foam flying right and left. He blundered once and I thought we were lost, but he recovered and an instant later was clattering up the farther slope. As we came out I heard the splash behind me as the first Prussian took the water. There was just the breadth of the Sambre between us.

I rode with my head sunk between my shoulders in Napoleon's fashion, and I did not dare to look back for fear they should see my moustache. I had turned up the collar of the grey coat so as partly to hide it. Even now if they found out their mistake they might turn and overtake the carriage. But when once we were on the road I could tell by the drumming of their hoofs how far distant they were, and it seemed to me that the sound grew perceptibly louder, as if they were slowly gaining upon me. We were riding now up the stony and rutted lane which led from the ford. I peeped back very cautiously from under my arm and I perceived that my danger came from a single rider, who was far ahead of his comrades. He was a Hussar, a very tiny fellow, upon a big black horse, and it was his light weight which had brought him into the foremost place. It is a place of honour; but it is also a place of danger, as he was soon to learn. I felt the holsters, but, to my horror, there were no pistols. There was a field-glass in one and the other was stuffed with papers. My sword had been left behind with Violette. Had I only my own weapons and my own little mare I could have played with these rascals. But I was not entirely unarmed. The Emperor's own sword hung to the saddle. It was curved and short, the hilt all crusted with gold – a thing more fitted to glitter at a review than to serve a soldier in his deadly need. I drew it, such as it was, and I waited my chance. Every instant the clink and clatter of the hoofs grew nearer. I heard the panting of the horse, and the fellow shouted some threat at me. There was a turn in the lane, and as I rounded it I drew up my white Arab on his haunches. As we spun round I met the Prussian Hussar face to face. He was going too fast to stop, and his only chance was to ride me down. Had he done so he might have met his own death, but he would have injured me or my horse past all hope of escape. But the fool flinched as he saw me waiting, and flew past me on my right. I lunged over my Arab's neck and buried my toy sword in his side. It must have been the finest steel and as sharp as a razor, for I hardly felt it enter, and yet his blood was within three inches of the hilt. His horse galloped on and he kept his saddle for a hundred yards before he sank down with his face on the mane, and then dived over the side of the neck on to the road. For my own part, I was already at his horse's heels. A few seconds had sufficed for all that I have told.

I heard the cry of rage and vengeance which rose from the Prussians as they passed their dead comrade, and I could not but smile as I wondered what they could think of the Emperor as a horseman and a swordsman. I glanced back cautiously as before, and I saw that none of the seven men stopped. The fate of their comrade was nothing compared to the carrying out of their mission. They were as untiring and as remorseless as bloodhounds. But I had a good lead, and the brave Arab was still going well. I thought that I was safe. And yet it was at that very instant that the most terrible danger befell me. The lane divided, and I took the smaller of the two divisions because it was the more grassy and the easier for the horse's hoofs. Imagine my horror when, riding through a gate, I found myself in a square of stables and farm-buildings, with no way out save that by which I had come! Ah, my friends, if my hair is snowy white, have I not had enough to make it so ?

To retreat was impossible. I could hear the thunder of the Prussians' hoofs in the lane. I looked round me, and Nature has blessed me with that quick eye which is the first of gifts to any soldier, but most of all to a leader of cavalry. Between a long, low line of stables and the farmhouse there was a pig-sty. Its front was made of bars of wood four feet high; the back was of stone, higher than the front. What was beyond I could not tell. The space between the front and the back was not more than a few yards. It was a desperate venture, and yet I must take it. Every instant the beating of those hurrying hoofs was louder and louder. I put my Arab at the pig-sty. He cleared the front beautifully, and came down with his forefeet upon the sleeping pig within, slipping forward upon his knees. I was thrown over the wall beyond, and fell upon my hands and face in a soft flower-bed. My horse was upon one side of the wall, I upon the other, and the Prussians were pouring into the yard. But I was up in an instant, and had seized the bridle of the plunging horse over the top of the wall. It was built of loose stones, and I dragged down a few of them to make a gap. As I tugged at the bridle and shouted the gallant creature rose to the leap, and an instant afterwards he was by my side and I with my foot on the stirrup.

An heroic idea had entered my mind as I mounted into the saddle. These Prussians, if they came over the pig-sty, could only come one at once, and their attack would not be formidable when they had not had time to recover from such a leap. Why should I not wait and kill them one by one as they came over? It was a glorious thought. They would learn that Etienne Gerard was not a safe man to hunt. My hand felt for my sword, but you can imagine my feelings, my friends, when I came upon an empty scabbard. It had been shaken out when the horse had tripped over that infernal pig. On what absurd trifles do our destinies hang – a pig on one side, Etienne Gerard on the other! Could I spring over the wall and get the sword? Impossible! The Prussians were already in the yard. I turned my Arab and resumed my flight.

But for a moment it seemed to me that I was in a far worse trap than before. I found myself in the garden of the farmhouse, an orchard in the centre and flower-beds all round. A high wall surrounded the whole place. I reflected, however, that there must be some point of entrance, since every visitor could not be expected to spring over the pig-sty. I rode round the wall. As I expected, I came upon a door with a key upon the inner side. I dismounted, unlocked it, opened it, and there was a Prussian Lancer sitting his horse within six feet of me.

For a moment we each stared at the other. Then I shut the door and locked it again. A crash and a cry came from the other end of the garden. I understood that one of my enemies had come to grief in trying to get over the pig-sty. How could I ever get out of this cul-de-sac? It was evident that some of the party had galloped round, while some had followed straight upon my tracks. Had I my sword I might· have beaten off the Lancer at the door, but to come out now was to be butchered. And yet if I waited some of them would certainly follow me on foot over the pig-sty, and what could I do then? I must act at once or I was lost. But it is at such moments that my wits are most active and my actions most prompt. Still leading my horse, I ran for a hundred yards by the side of the wall away from the spot where the Lancer was watching. There I stopped, and with an effort I tumbled down several of the loose stones from the top of the wall. The instant I had done so I hurried back to the door. As I expected, he thought I was making a gap for my escape at that point, and I heard the thud of his horse's hoofs as he galloped to cut me off. As I reached the gate I looked back, and I saw a green-coated horseman, whom I knew to be Count Stein, clear the pig-sty and gallop furiously with a shout of triumph across the garden. 'Surrender, your Majesty, surrender!' he yelled; 'we will give you quarter!' I slipped through the gate, but had no time to lock it on the other side. Stein was at my very heels, and the Lancer had already turned his horse. Springing upon my Arab's back, I was off once more with a clear stretch of grass land before me. Stein had to dismount to open the gate, to lead his horse through, and to mount again before he could follow. It was he that I feared rather than the Lancer, whose horse was coarse-bred and weary. I galloped hard for a mile before I ventured to look back, and then Stein was a musket-shot from me, and the Lancer as much again, while only three of the others were in sight. My nine Prussians were coming down to more manageable numbers, and yet one was too much for an unarmed man.

It had surprised me that during this long chase I had seen no fugitives from the army, but I reflected that I was considerably to the west of their line of flight, and that I must edge more towards the east if I wished to join them. Unless I did so it was probable that my pursuers, even if they could not overtake me themselves, would keep me in view until I was headed off by some of their comrades coming from the north. As I looked to the eastward I saw afar off a line of dust which stretched for miles across the country. This was certainly the main road along which our unhappy army was flying. But I soon had proof that some of our stragglers had wandered into these side tracks, for I came suddenly upon a horse grazing at the corner of a field, and beside him, with his back against the bank, his master, a French Cuirassier, terribly wounded and evidently at the point of death. I sprang down, seized his long, heavy sword, and rode on with it. Never shall I forget the poor man's face as he looked at me with his failing sight. He was an old, grey-moustached soldier, one of the real fanatics, and to him this last vision of his Emperor was like a revelation from on high. Astonishment, love, pride – all shone in his pallid face. He said something – I fear they were his last words – but I had no time to listen, and I galloped on my way.

All this time I had been on the meadow-land, which was intersected in this part by broad ditches. Some of them could not have been less than from fourteen to fifteen feet, and my heart was in my mouth as I went at each of them, for a slip would have been my ruin. But whoever selected the Emperor's horses had done his work well. The creature, save when it balked on the bank of the Sambre, never failed me for an instant. We cleared everything in one stride. And yet we could not shake off those infernal Prussians. As I left each watercourse behind me I looked back with renewed hope, but it was only to see Stein on his white-legged chestnut flying over it as lightly as I had done myself. He was my enemy, but I honoured him for the way in which he carried himself that day.

Again and again I measured the distance which separated him from the next horseman. I had the idea that I might turn and cut him down, as I had the Hussar, before his comrade could come to his help. But the others had closed up and were not far behind. I reflected that this Stein was probably as fine a swordsman as he was a rider, and that it might take me some little time to get the better of him. In that case the others would come to his aid and I should be lost. On the whole, it was wiser to continue my flight.

A road with poplars on either side ran across the plain from east to west. It would lead me towards the long line of dust which marked the French retreat. I wheeled my horse, therefore, and galloped down it. As I rode I saw a single house in front of me upon the right, with a great bush hung over the door to mark it as an inn. Outside there were several peasants, but for them I cared nothing. What frightened me was to see the gleam of a red coat, which showed that there were British in the place. However, I could not turn and I could not stop, so there was nothing for it but to gallop on and to take my chance. There were no troops in sight, so these men must be stragglers or marauders, from whom I had little to fear. As I approached I saw that there were two of them sitting drinking on a bench outside the inn door. I saw them stagger to their feet, and it was evident that they were both very drunk. One stood swaying in the middle of the road. 'It's Boney! So help me, it's Boney!' he yelled. He ran with his hands out to catch me, but luckily for himself his drunken feet stumbled and he fell on his face in the road. The other was more dangerous. He had rushed into the inn, and just as I passed I saw him run out with his musket in his hand. He dropped upon one knee, and I stooped forward over my horse's neck. A single shot from a Prussian or an Austrian is a small matter, but the British were at that time the best shots in Europe, and my drunkard seemed steady enough when he had a gun at his shoulder. I heard the crack, and my horse gave a convulsive spring which would have unseated many a rider. For an instant I thought he was killed, but when I turned in my saddle I saw a stream of blood running down the off hind-quarter. I looked back at the Englishman, and the brute had bitten the end off another cartridge and was ramming it into his musket, but before he had it primed we were beyond his range. These men were foot-soldiers and could not join in the chase, but I heard them whooping and tally-hoing behind me as if I had been a fox. The peasants also shouted and ran through the fields flourishing their sticks. From all sides I heard cries, and everywhere were the rushing, waving figures of my pursuers. To think of the great Emperor being chivied over the countryside in this fashion! It made me long to have these rascals within the sweep of my sword.

But now I felt that I was nearing the end of my course. I had done all that a man could be expected to do – some would say more – but at last I had come to a point from which I could see no escape. The horses of my pursuers were exhausted, but mine was exhausted and wounded also. It was losing blood fast, and we left a red trail upon the white, dusty road. Already his pace was slackening, and sooner or later he must drop under me. I looked back, and there were the five inevitable Prussians – Stein, a hundred yards in front, then a Lancer, and then three others riding together. Stein had drawn his sword, and he waved it at me. For my own part I was determined not to give myself up. I would try how many of these Prussians I could take with me into the other world. At this supreme moment all the great deeds of my life rose in a vision before me, and I felt that this, my last exploit, was indeed a worthy close to such a career. My death would be a fatal blow to those who loved me, to my dear mother, to my Hussars, to others who shall be nameless. But all of them had my honour and my fame at heart, and I felt that their grief would be tinged with pride when they learned how I had ridden and how I had fought upon this last day. Therefore I hardened my heart and, as my Arab limped more and more upon his wounded leg, I drew the great sword which I had taken from the Cuirassier, and I set my teeth for my supreme struggle. My hand was in the very act of tightening the bridle, for I feared that if I delayed longer I might find myself on foot fighting against five mounted men. At that instant my eye fell upon something which brought hope to my heart and a shout of joy to my lips.

From a grove of trees in front of me there projected the steeple of a village church. But there could not be two steeples like that, for the corner of it had crumbled away or been struck by lightning, so that it was of a most fantastic shape. I had seen it only two days before, and it was the church of the village of Gosselies. It was not the hope of reaching the village which set my heart singing with joy, but it was that I knew my ground now, and that farmhouse not half a mile ahead, with its gable end sticking out from amid the trees, must be that very farm of St Aunay where we had bivouacked, and which I had named to Captain Sabbatier as the rendezvous of the Hussars of Conflans. There they were, my little rascals, if I could but reach them. With every bound my horse grew weaker. Each instant the sound of the pursuit grew louder. I heard a gust of crackling German oaths at my very heels. A pistol bullet sighed in my ears. Spurring frantically and beating my poor Arab with the flat of my sword I kept him at the top of his speed. The open gate of the farmyard lay before me. I saw the twinkle of steel within. Stein's horse's head was within ten yards of me as I thundered through. 'To me, comrades! To me!' I yelled. I heard a buzz as when the angry bees swarm from their nest. Then my splendid white Arab fell dead under me, and I was hurled on to the cobble-stones of the yard, where I can remember no more.

Such was my last and most famous exploit, my dear friends, a story which rang through Europe and has made the name of Etienne Gerard famous in history. Alas! that all my efforts could only give the Emperor a few weeks more liberty, since he surrendered upon July 15th to the English.

But it was not my fault that he was not able to collect the forces still waiting for him in France, and to fight another Waterloo with a happier ending. Had others been as loyal as I was the history of the world might have been changed, the Emperor would have preserved his throne, and such a soldier as I would not have been left to spend his life in planting cabbages or to while away his old age telling stories in a café. You ask me about the fate of Stein and the Prussian horsemen! Of the three who dropped upon the way I know nothing. One you will remember that I killed. There remained five, three of whom were cut down by my Hussars, who, for the instant, were under the impression that it was indeed the Emperor whom they were defending. Stein was taken, slightly wounded, and so was one of the Uhlans. The truth was not told to them, for we thought it best that no news, or false news, should get about as to where the Emperor was, so that Count Stein still believed that he was within a few yards of making that tremendous capture. 'You may well love and honour your Emperor,' said he, 'for such a horseman and such a swordsman I have never seen.' He could not understand why the young colonel of Hussars laughed so heartily at his words – but he has learned since.

8 The last adventure of the Brigadier

I will tell you no more stories, my dear friends. It is said that man is like the hare, which runs in a circle and comes back to die at the point from which it started. Gascony has been calling to me of late. I see the blue Garonne winding among the vineyards and the bluer ocean towards which its waters sweep. I see the old town also, and the bristle of masts from the side of the long stone quay. My heart hungers for the breath of my native air and the warm glow of my native sun. Here in Paris are my friends, my occupations, my pleasures. There all who have known me are in their grave. And yet the south-west wind as it rattles on my windows seems always to be the strong voice of the mother-land calling her child back to that bosom into which I am ready to sink. I have played my part in my time. The time has passed. I must pass also. Nay, dear friends, do not look sad, for what can be happier than a life completed in honour and made beautiful with friendship and love? And yet it is solemn also when a man approaches the end of the long road and sees the turning which leads him into the unknown. But the Emperor and all his Marshals have ridden round that dark turning and passed into the beyond. My Hussars, too – there are not fifty men who are not waiting yonder. I must go. But on this the last night I will tell you that which is more than a tale – it is a great historical secret. My lips have been sealed, but I see no reason why I should not leave behind me some account of this remarkable adventure, which must otherwise be entirely lost, since I, and only I of all living men, have a knowledge of the facts.

I will ask you to go back with me to the year 1821. In that year our great Emperor had been absent from us for six years, and only now and then from over the seas we heard some whisper which showed that he was still alive. You cannot think what a weight it was upon our hearts for us who loved him to think of him in captivity eating his giant soul out upon that lonely island. From the moment we rose until we closed our eyes in sleep the thought was always with us, and we felt dishonoured that he, our chief and master, should be so humiliated without our being able to move a hand to help him. There were many who would most willingly have laid down the remainder of their lives to bring him a little ease, and yet all that we could do was to sit and grumble in our cafés and stare at the map, counting up the leagues of water which lay between us. It seemed that he might have been in the moon for all that we could do to help him. But that was only because we were all soldiers and knew nothing of the sea.

Of course, we had our own little troubles to make us bitter, as well as the wrongs of our Emperor. There were many of us who had held high rank and would hold it again if he came back to his own. We had not found it possible to take service under the white flag of the Bourbons, or to take an oath which might turn our sabres against the man whom we loved. So we found ourselves with neither work nor money. What could we do save gather together and gossip and grumble, while those who had a little paid the score and those who had nothing shared the bottle ? Now and then, if we were lucky, we managed to pick a quarrel with one of the Garde du Corps, and if we left him on his back in the Bois we felt that we had struck a blow for Napoleon once again. They came to know our haunts in time, and they avoided them as if they had been hornets' nests.

There was one of these – the Sign of the Great Man – in the Rue Varennes, which was frequented by several of the more distinguished and younger Napoleonic officers. Nearly all of us had been colonels or aides-de-camp, and when any man of less distinction came among us we generally made him feel that he had taken a liberty. There were Captain Lepine, who had won the medal of honour at Leipzig; Colonel Bonnet, aide-de-camp to Macdonald; Colonel Jourdan, whose fame in the army was hardly second to my own; Sabbatier of my own Hussars, Meunier of the Red

Lancers, Le Breton of the Guards, and a dozen others. Every night we met and talked, played dominoes, drank a glass or two and wondered how long it would be before the Emperor would be back and we at the head of our regiments once more. The Bourbons had already lost any hold they ever had upon the country, as was shown a few years afterwards, when Paris rose against them and they were hunted for the third time out of France. Napoleon had but to show himself on the coast, and he would have marched without firing a musket to the capital, exactly as he had done when he came back from Elba.

Well, when affairs were in this state there arrived one night in February, in our café, a most singular little man. He was short but exceedingly broad, with huge shoulders, and a head which was a deformity, so large was it. His heavy brown face was scarred with white streaks in a most extraordinary manner, and he had grizzled whiskers such as seamen wear. Two gold ear-rings in his ears, and plentiful tattooing upon his hands and arms, told us also that he was of the sea before he introduced himself to us as Captain Fourneau, of the Emperor's navy. He had letters of introduction to two of our number, and there could be no doubt that he was devoted to the cause. He won our respect, too, for he had seen as much fighting as any of us, and the burns upon his face were caused by his standing to his post upon the *Orient*, at the Battle of the Nile, until the vessel blew up underneath him. Yet he would say little about himself, but he sat in the corner of the café watching us all with a wonderfully sharp pair of eyes and listening intently to our talk.

One night I was leaving the café when Captain Fourneau followed me, and touching me on the arm he led me without saying a word for some distance until we reached his lodgings. 'I wish to have a chat with you,' said he, and so conducted me up the stair to his room. There he lit a lamp and handed me a sheet of paper which he took from an envelope in his bureau. It was dated a few months before from the Palace of Schönbrunn at Vienna. 'Captain Fourneau is acting in the highest interests of the Emperor Napoleon.

Those who love the Emperor should obey him without question – Marie Louise.' That is what I read. I was familiar with the signature of the Empress, and I could not doubt that this was genuine.

'Well,' said he, 'are you satisfied as to my credentials ?'

'Entirely.'

'Are you prepared to take your orders from me ?'

'This document leaves me no choice.'

'Good! In the first place, I understand from something you said in the café that you can speak English ?'

'Yes, I can.'

'Let me hear you do so.'

I said in English, 'Whenever the Emperor needs the help of Etienne Gerard, I am ready night and day to give my life in his service.'

Captain Fourneau smiled.

'It is funny English,' said he, 'but still it is better than no English. For my own part I speak English like an Englishman. It is all that I have to show for six years spent in an English prison. Now I will tell you why I have come to Paris. I have come in order to choose an agent who will help me in a matter which affects the interests of the Emperor. I was told that it was at the café of the Great Man that I would find the pick of his old officers, and that I could rely upon every man there being devoted to his interests. I studied you all, therefore, and I have come to the conclusion that you are the one who is most suited for my purpose.'

I acknowledged the compliment. 'What is it that you wish me to do ?' I asked.

'Merely to keep me company for a few months,' said he. 'You must know that after my release in England I settled down there, married an English wife, and rose to command a small English merchant ship, in which I have made several voyages from Southampton to the Guinea coast. They look on me there as an Englishman. You can understand, however, that with my feelings about the Emperor I am lonely sometimes, and that it would be an advantage to me to have a companion who would sympathize with my thoughts. One gets very bored on these long voyages, and I would make it worth your while to share my cabin.'

He looked hard at me with his shrewd grey eyes all the time that he was uttering this rigmarole, and I gave him a glance in return which showed him that he was not dealing with a fool. He took out a canvas bag full of money.

'There are a hundred pounds in gold in this bag,' said he. 'You will be able to buy some comforts for your voyage. I should recommend you to get them in Southampton, whence we will start in ten days. The name of the vessel is the *Black Swan*. I return to Southampton tomorrow, and I shall hope to see you in the course of next week.'

'Come now,' said I, 'tell me frankly what is the destination of our voyage?'

'Oh, didn't I tell you?' he answered. 'We are bound for the Guinea coast of Africa.'

'Then how can that be in the highest interests of the Emperor?' I asked.

'It is in his highest interests that you ask no indiscreet questions and I give no indiscreet replies,' he answered, sharply. So he brought the interview to an end, and I found myself back in my lodgings with nothing save this bag of gold to show that this singular interview had indeed taken place.

There was every reason why I should see the adventure to a conclusion, and so within a week I was on my way to England. I passed from St Malo to Southampton, and on inquiry at the docks I had no difficulty in finding the *Black Swan*, a neat little vessel of a shape which is called, as I learned afterwards, a brig. There was Captain Fourneau himself upon the deck, and seven or eight rough fellows hard at work grooming her and making her ready for sea. He greeted me and led me down to his cabin.

'You are plain Mr Gerard now,' said he, 'and a Channel Islander. I would be obliged to you if you would kindly forget your military ways and drop your cavalry swagger when you walk up and down my deck. A beard, too, would seem more sailor-like than those moustaches.'

I was horrified by his words, but, after all, there are no ladies on the high seas, and what did it matter ? He rang for the steward.

'Gustav,' said he, 'you will pay every attention to my friend, Monsieur Etienne Gerard, who makes this voyage with us. This is Gustav Kerouan, my Breton steward,' he explained, 'and you are very safe in his hands.'

This steward, with his harsh face and stern eyes, looked a very warlike person for so peaceful an employment. I said nothing, however, though you may guess that I kept my eyes open. A berth had been prepared for me next the cabin, which would have seemed comfortable enough had it not contrasted with the extraordinary splendour of Fourneau's quarters. He was certainly a most luxurious person, for his room was new-fitted with velvet and silver in a way which would have suited the yacht of a noble better than a little West African trader. So thought the mate, Mr Burns, who could not hide his amusement and contempt whenever he looked at it. This fellow, a big, solid red-headed Englishman, had the other berth connected with the cabin. There was a second mate named Turner, who lodged in the middle of the ship, and there were nine men and one boy in the crew, three of whom, as I was informed by Mr Burns, were Channel Islanders like myself. This Burns, the first mate, was much interested to know why I was coming with them.

'I come for pleasure,' said I.

He stared at me.

'Ever been to the West Coast ?' he asked.

I said that I had not.

'I thought not,' said he. 'You'll never come again for that reason, anyhow.'

Some three days after my arrival we untied the ropes by which the ship was tethered and we set off upon our journey. I was never a good sailor, and I may confess that we were far out of sight of any land before I was able to venture upon deck. At last, however, upon the fifth day I drank the soup which the good Kerouan brought me, and I was able to crawl from my bunk and up the stair. The fresh air revived me, and from that time onwards I accommodated myself to the motion of the vessel. My beard had begun to grow also, and I have no doubt that I should have made as fine a sailor as I have a soldier had I chanced to be born to that branch of the service. I learned to pull the ropes which hoisted the sails, and also to haul round the long sticks to which they are attached. For the most part, however, my duties were to play écarté with Captain Fourneau, and to act as his companion. It was not strange that he should need one, for neither of his mates could read nor write, though each of them was an excellent seaman. If our captain had died suddenly I cannot imagine how we should have found our way in that waste of waters, for it was only he who had the knowledge which enabled him to mark our place upon the chart. He had this fixed upon the cabin wall, and every day he put our course upon it so that we could see at a glance how far we were from our destination. It was wonderful how well he could calculate it, for one morning he said that we should see the Cape Verd light that very night, and there it was, sure enough, upon our left front the moment that darkness came. Next day, however, the land was out of sight, and Burns, the mate, explained to me that we should see no more until we came to our port in the Gulf of Biafra. Every day we flew south with a favouring wind, and always at noon the pin upon the chart was moved nearer and nearer to the African coast. I may explain that palm oil was the cargo which we were in search of, and that our own lading consisted of coloured cloths, old muskets, and such other trifles as the English sell to the savages.

At last the wind which had followed us so long died away, and for several days we drifted about on a calm and oily sea under a sun which brought the pitch bubbling out between the planks upon the deck. We turned and turned our sails to catch every wandering puff, until at last we came out of this belt of calm and ran south again with a brisk breeze, the sea all round us being alive with flying fishes. For some days Burns appeared to be uneasy, and I observed him continually shading his eyes with his hand and staring at the horizon as if he were looking for land. Twice I caught him with his red head against the chart in the cabin, gazing at that pin, which was always approaching and yet never reaching the African coast. At last one evening, as Captain Fourneau and I were playing écarté in the cabin, the mate entered with an angry look upon his sunburned face.

'I beg your pardon, Captain Fourneau,' said he. 'But do you know what course the man at the wheel is steering?'

'Due south,' the captain answered, with his eyes fixed upon his cards.

'And he should be steering due east.'

'How do you make that out?'

The mate gave an angry growl.

'I may not have much education,' said he, 'but let me tell you this, Captain Fourneau, I've sailed these waters since I was a little nipper of ten, and I know the line when I'm on it, and I know the doldrums, and I know how to find my way to the oil rivers. We are south of the line now, and we should be steering due east instead of due south if your port is the port that the owners sent you to.'

'Excuse me, Mr Gerard. Just remember that it is my lead,' said the captain, laying down his cards. 'Come to the map here, Mr Burns, and I will give you a lesson in practical navigation. Here is the trade wind from the south-west and here is the line, and here is the port that we want to make, and here is a man who will have his own way aboard his own ship.' As he spoke he seized the unfortunate mate by the throat and squeezed him until he was nearly senseless. Kerouan, the steward, had rushed in with a rope, and between them they gagged and trussed the man, so that he was utterly helpless.

'There is one of our Frenchmen at the wheel. We had best put the mate overboard,' said the steward.

'That is safest,' said Captain Fourneau.

But that was more than I could stand. Nothing would persuade me to agree to the death of a helpless man. With a bad grace Captain Fourneau consented to spare him, and we carried him to the after-hold, which lay under the cabin.

There he was laid among the bales of Manchester cloth.

'It is not worth while to put down the hatch,' said Captain Fourneau. 'Gustav, go to Mr Turner, and tell him that I would like to have a word with him.'

The unsuspecting second mate entered the cabin, and was instantly gagged and secured as Burns had been. He was carried down and laid beside his comrade. The hatch was then replaced.

'Our hands have been forced by that red-headed dolt,' said the captain, 'and I have had to explode my mine before I wished. However, there is no great harm done, and it will not seriously disarrange my plans. Kerouan, you will take a keg of rum forward to the crew and tell them that the captain gives it to them to drink his health on the occasion of crossing the line. They will know no better. As to our own fellows, bring them down to your pantry so that we may be sure that they are ready for business. Now, Colonel Gerard, with your permission we will resume our game of écarté.'

It is one of those occasions which one does not forget. This captain, who was a man of iron, shuffled and cut, dealt and played as if he were in his café. From below we heard the inarticulate murmurings of the two mates, half smothered by the handkerchiefs which gagged them. Outside the timbers creaked and the sails hummed under the brisk breeze which was sweeping us upon our way. Amid the splash of the waves and the whistle of the wind we heard the wild cheers and shoutings of the English sailors as they broached the keg of rum. We played half a dozen games, and then the captain rose. 'I think they are ready for us now,' said he. He took a brace of pistols from a locker, and he handed one of them to me.

But we had no need to fear resistance, for there was no one to resist. The Englishman of those days, whether soldier or sailor, was an incorrigible drunkard. Without drink he was a brave and good man. But if drink were laid before him it was a perfect madness – nothing could induce him to take it with moderation. In the dim light of the den which they inhabited, five senseless figures and two shouting, swearing, singing madmen represented the crew of the *Black Swan*. Coils of rope were brought forward by the steward, and with the help of two French seamen (the third was at the wheel) we secured the drunkards and tied them up, so that it was impossible for them to speak or move. They were placed under the fore-hatch, as their officers had been under the after one, and Kerouan was directed twice a day to give them food and drink. So at last we found that the *Black Swan* was entirely our own.

Had there been bad weather I do not know what we should have done, but we still went gaily upon our way with a wind which was strong enough to drive us swiftly south, but not strong enough to cause us alarm. On the evening of the third day I found Captain Fourneau gazing eagerly out from the platform in the front of the vessel. 'Look, Gerard, look!' he cried and pointed over the pole which struck out in front.

A light blue sky rose from a dark blue sea, and far away, at the point where they met, was a shadowy something like a cloud, but more definite in shape.

'What is it?' I cried.

'It is land.'

'And what land?'

I strained my ears for the answer, and yet I knew already what the answer would be.

'It is St Helena.'

Here, then, was the island of my dreams! Here was the cage where our great Eagle of France was confined! All those thousands of leagues of water had not sufficed to keep Gerard from the master whom he loved. There he was, there on that cloud-bank yonder over the dark blue sea. How my eyes devoured it! How my soul flew in front of the vessel – flew on and on to tell him that he was not forgotten, that after many days one faithful servant was coming to his side! Every instant the dark blur upon the water grew harder and clearer. Soon I could see plainly enough that it was indeed a mountainous island. The night fell, but still I knelt upon the deck, with my eyes fixed upon the darkness which covered the spot where I knew that the great Emperor was. An hour passed and another one, and then suddenly a little golden twinkling light shone out exactly ahead of us. It was the light of the window of some house – perhaps of his house. It could not be more than a mile or two away. Oh, how I held out my hands to it! – they were the hands of Etienne Gerard, but it was for all France that they were held out.

Every light had been extinguished aboard our ship, and presently, at the direction of Captain Fourneau, we all pulled upon one of the ropes, which had the effect of swinging round one of the sticks above us, and so stopping the vessel. Then he asked me to step down to the cabin.

'You understand everything now, Colonel Gerard,' said he, 'and you will forgive me if I did not take you into my complete confidence before. In a matter of such importance I make no man my confidant. I have long planned the rescue of the Emperor, and my remaining in England and joining their merchant service was entirely with that design. All has worked out exactly as I expected. I have made several successful voyages to the West Coast of Africa, so that there was no difficulty in my obtaining the command of this one. One by one I got these old French man-of-war's men among the hands. As to you, I was anxious to have one tried fighting man in case of resistance, and I also desired to have a fitting companion for the Emperor during his long homeward voyage. My cabin is already fitted up for his use. I trust that before tomorrow morning he will be inside it, and we out of sight of this accursed island.'

You can think of my emotion, my friends, as I listened to these words. I embraced the brave Fourneau, and implored him to tell me how I could assist him.

'I must leave it all in your hands,' said he. 'Would that I could have been the first to pay him homage, but it would not be wise for me to go. The glass is falling, there is a storm brewing, and we have the land under our lee. Besides, there are three English cruisers near the island which may be upon us at any moment. It is for me, therefore, to guard the ship and for you to bring off the Emperor.'

I thrilled at the words.

'Give me your instructions!' I cried.

'I can only spare you one man, for already I can hardly pull round the yards,' said he. 'One of the boats has been lowered, and this man will row you ashore and await your return. The light which you see is indeed the light of Longwood. All who are in the house are your friends, and all may be depended upon to aid the Emperor's escape. There is a cordon of English sentries, but they are not very near to the house. Once you have got as far as that you will convey our plans to the Emperor, guide him down to the boat, and bring him on board.'

The Emperor himself could not have given his instructions more shortly and clearly. There was not a moment to be lost. The boat with the seaman was waiting alongside. I stepped into it, and an instant afterwards we had pushed off. Our little boat danced over the dark waters, but always shining before my eyes was the light of Longwood, the light of the Emperor, the star of hope. Presently the bottom of the boat grated upon the pebbles of the beach. It was a deserted cove, and no challenge from a sentry came to disturb us. I left the seaman by the boat and began to climb the hillside.

There was a goat-track winding in and out among the rocks, so I had no difficulty in finding my way. It stands to reason that all paths in St Helena would lead to the Emperor. I came to a gate. No sentry – and I passed through. Another gate – still no sentry! I wondered what had become of this cordon of which Fourneau had spoken. I had come now to the top of my climb, for there was the light burning steadily right in front of me. I concealed myself and took a good look round, but still I could see no sign of the enemy. As I approached I saw the house, a long, low building with a veranda. A man was walking up and down upon the path in front. I crept nearer and had a look at him. Perhaps it was this cursed Hudson Lowe. What a triumph if I could not only rescue the Emperor, but also avenge him! But it was more likely that this man was an English sentry. I crept nearer still, and the man stopped in front of the lighted window, so that I could see him. No; it was no soldier, but a priest. I wondered what such a man could be doing there at two in the morning. Was he French or English? If he were one of the household I might take him into my confidence. If he were English he might ruin all my plans. I crept a little nearer still, and at that moment he entered the house, a flood of light pouring out through the open door. All was clear for me now, and I understood that not an instant was to be lost. Bending myself double I ran swiftly forward to the lighted window. Raising my head I peeped through, and there was the Emperor lying dead before me!

My friends, I fell down upon the gravel walk as senseless as if a bullet had passed through my brain. So great was the shock that I wonder that I survived it. And yet in half an hour I had staggered to my feet again, shivering in every limb, my teeth chattering, and there I stood staring with the eyes of a maniac into that room of death.

He lay upon a bier in the centre of the chamber, calm, composed, majestic, his face full of that reserve power which lightened our hearts upon the day of battle. A half-smile was fixed upon his pale lips, and his eyes, half-opened, seemed to be turned on mine. He was stouter than when I had seen him at Waterloo, and there was a gentleness of expression which I had never seen in life. On either side of him burned rows of candles, and this was the beacon which had welcomed us at sea, which had guided me over the water, and which I had hailed as my star of hope. Dimly I became conscious that many people were kneeling in the room; the little Court, men and women, who had shared his fortunes, Bertrand, his wife, the priest, Montholon – all were there. I would have prayed too, but my heart was too heavy and bitter for prayer. And yet I must leave, and I could not leave him without a sign. Regardless of whether I was seen or not, I drew myself erect before my dead leader, brought my heels together, and raised my hand in a last salute. Then I turned and hurried off through the darkness, with the picture of the wan, smiling lips and the steady grey eyes dancing always before me.

It had seemed to me but a little time that I had been away, and yet the boatman told me that it was hours. Only when he spoke of it did I observe that the wind was blowing half a gale from the sea and that the waves were roaring in upon the beach. Twice we tried to push out our little boat, and twice it was thrown back by the sea. The third time a great wave filled it and stove the bottom. Helplessly we waited beside it until the dawn broke, to show a raging sea and a flying scud above it. There was no sign of the *Black Swan*. Climbing the hill we looked down, but on all the great torn expanse of the ocean there was no gleam of a sail. She was gone. Whether she had sunk, or whether she was recaptured by her English crew, or what strange fate may have been in store for her, I do not know. Never again in this life did I see Captain Fourneau to tell him the result of my mission. For my own part I gave myself up to the English, my boatman and I pretending that we were the only survivors of a lost vessel – though, indeed, there was no pretence in the matter. At the hands of their officers I received that generous hospitality which I have always encountered, but it was many a long month before I could get a passage back to the dear land outside of which there can be no happiness for so true a Frenchman as myself.

And so I tell you in one evening how I bade good-bye to my master, and I take my leave also of you, my kind friends, who have listened so patiently to the long-winded stories of an old broken soldier. Russia, Italy, Germany, Spain, Portugal, and England, you have gone with me to all these countries, and you have seen through my dim eyes something of the sparkle and splendour of those great days, and I have brought back to you some shadow of those men whose tread shook the earth. Treasure it in your minds and pass it on to your children, for the memory of a great age is the most precious treasure that a nation can possess. As the tree is nurtured by its own cast leaves, so it is these dead men and vanished days which may bring out another blossoming of heroes, of rulers, and of sages. I go to Gascony, but my words stay here in your memory, and long after Etienne Gerard is forgotten a heart may be warmed or a spirit braced by some faint echo of the words that he has spoken. Gentlemen, an old soldier salutes you and bids you farewell.

Sir Arthur Conan Doyle

The Exploits of Brigadier Gerard 70p

Etienne Gerard, idol of the ladies, best horseman and surest blade in
Napoleon's ten regiments of hussars, has the stoutest heart (and the
thickest head) in the Grand Army.
His remarkable adventures with Spanish guerillas, Corsican assassins,
German patriots and English milords always spring from a happy
blend of chance and circumstance. For Chance is a woman and loves to
keep an eye on a gallant hussar.

Sir Nigel 75p

In this tale of honour, conquest and adventure, the French wars of the
fourteenth century are brought vividly to life. Before young Nigel
Loring sets forth to France as Squire to the noble Sir John Chandos, he
makes a solemn lover's vow that he will not return until he has
accomplished three great deeds of honour.
The story of how he fulfils his vow in battles, duels and tourneys makes
a stirring and thrilling chronicle of valour.

The White Company 75p

Battle-royal, tourney, mêlée, skirmish or siege – all were one to the
hard-bitten mercenaries of the White Company. At close quarters they
are feared as much for their belligerent and unashamed patriotism as for
their ability to fight like devils – to the death, if need be.
Led by the renowned Sir Nigel Loring, their valorous adventures, as
they wage their honour and their lives against the French, brilliantly
recapture the robust flavour of the fourteenth century, and of England
in the making.

The Adventures of Sherlock Holmes 75p

With an introduction by Eric Ambler
This volume contains some of Sherlock Holmes' most famous cases, in which his eagle eye and brilliant brain are stretched to their limits.

The Return of Sherlock Holmes 75p

With an introduction by Angus Wilson
Assumed dead after his terrible struggle with master criminal Moriarty high above the Reichenbach Falls. Sherlock Holmes astonishes the world yet again by returning to tell the story of his extraordinary escape, and to embark on more fascinating exploits.

Also available
His Last Bow   60p
The Hound of the Baskervilles 50p
A Study in Scarlet   50p
The Valley of Fear   50p
The Sign of Four   50p

John Gardner
Moriarty   75p

Thursday 5 April 1894 . . . Arch-enemy of Sherlock Holmes, Professor Moriarty returns from the grave to repossess his criminal empire. From his Limehouse stronghold he deals savagely and in chilling fashion with would-be rivals, dupes the police, plots the theft of the Crown Jewels and writes *finis* to Jack the Ripper.

Selected bestsellers

☐ **The Eagle Has Landed** Jack Higgins 80p
☐ **The Moneychangers** Arthur Hailey 95p
☐ **Marathon Man** William Goldman 70p
☐ **Nightwork** Irwin Shaw 75p
☐ **Tropic of Ruislip** Leslie Thomas 75p
☐ **One Flew Over The Cuckoo's Nest** Ken Kesey 75p
☐ **Collision** Spencer Dunmore 70p
☐ **Perdita's Prince** Jean Plaidy 70p
☐ **The Eye of the Tiger** Wilbur Smith 80p
☐ **The Shootist** Glendon Swarthout 60p
☐ **Of Human Bondage** Somerset Maugham 95p
☐ **Rebecca** Daphne du Maurier 80p
☐ **Slay Ride** Dick Francis 60p
☐ **Jaws** Peter Benchley 70p
☐ **Let Sleeping Vets Lie** James Herriot 60p
☐ **If Only They Could Talk** James Herriot 60p
☐ **It Shouldn't Happen to a Vet** James Herriot 60p
☐ **Vet in Harness** James Herriot 60p
☐ **Tinker Tailor Soldier Spy** John le Carré 75p
☐ **Gone with the Wind** Margaret Mitchell £1·75
☐ **Cashelmara** Susan Howatch £1·25
☐ **The Nonesuch** Georgette Heyer 60p
☐ **The Grapes of Wrath** John Steinbeck 95p
☐ **Drum** Kyle Onstott 60p

All these books are available at your bookshop or newsagent;
or can be obtained direct from the publisher
Just tick the titles you want and fill in the form below
Prices quoted are applicable in UK
Pan Books, Cavaye Place, London SW10 9PG
Send purchase price plus 15p for the first book and 5p for each
additional book, to allow for postage and packing

Name————————————————————
(block letters please)

Address ————————————————————

————————————————————